AROUND THE WORLD IN 80 RECORD STORES

Published in 2018 by Dog 'n' Bone Books
An imprint of Ryland Peters & Small Ltd
20–21 Jockey's Fields   341 E 116th St
London WC1R 4BW   New York, NY 10029

www.rylandpeters.com

10 9 8 7 6 5 4 3 2 1

A CIP catalog record for this book is available from
the Library of Congress and the British Library.

ISBN: 978 1 911026 60 0

Printed in China

Editor: Caroline West
Designer: Eoghan O'Brien
Photography credits: page 8 Jeff Gilbert/Alamy;
13 James McCauley/HMV; 15 Marcus Barnes; 20 Keith
Morris/Getty; 21 E.Westmacott/Alamy; 35 Mark Dix;
48–9 Ovidiu Stanciu; 62 Hemis/Alamy (top left) and
Liz Eve/ArcaidImages/Getty (top right and bottom);
66–7 Public Possession; 98 David L. Moore - JPN/
Alamy; 104 Paul Quayle/Alamy; 108 W. G. Murray/
Alamy; 109 LHB Photo/Alamy; 122 Kim Karpeles/
Alamy; 124 Ed Rooney/Alamy

The publishers would like to thank all the record
stores, owners, and staff who kindly took the time
to provide images to feature in this book.

AROUND THE WORLD IN 80 RECORD STORES

MARCUS BARNES

A GUIDE TO THE BEST VINYL EMPORIUMS ON THE PLANET

DOG 'N' BONE

Contents

Introduction

Record stores can be very special places when created with love, care, and attention. Record collecting is a hobby that requires dedication, commitment, a keen eye (and ear), and an unwavering passion for music in its physical form. So, of course, most shops are run by vinyl enthusiasts, people who understand what it means to be a true lover of black wax. This means these temples of vinyl are often curated in such a way as to facilitate the discovery and collection of records, making it as smooth and easy as possible for their customers to find what they want. Good record shops help buyers to uncover new music and artists, and always maintain a relaxed vibe that allows collectors to feel confident enough to ask for help if they need it. The very best record stores not only have all these key characteristics, but also become local institutions, supplying the surrounding area with music, inspiring up-and-coming artists, and forming a community around the shops themselves, while at the same time cultivating a symbiotic relationship with the local music scene as one feeds into the other and vice versa.

In today's highly connected world, the greatest record stores attain global reputation which makes them tourist hubs, transcending their locality to stretch out across the planet and attract customers from every single continent on Earth. The most celebrated examples establish their own identity, putting their own spin on the traditional record shop

JH-1980-S

JAZZHOLE

Lagos

HAPPYFEET

PRAGUE

SPR 2009

RLR-2012

RED LIGHT RECORDS

Amsterdam

DIG-2007

DIG

SOUNDSTATION · COPENHAGEN

SS-1991

MOSCOW

RADIATION RECORDS

Rome

▼

Spillers

EST-1894

ATOM HEART

THE RECORD EXCHANGE

MONTREAL

CARDIFF

· BRISBANE ·

HEAR RECORDS

SINGAPORE

THE THING

NEW YORK CITY

archetype and they also welcome the novice. A crucial aspect of a successful vinyl vendor is to create an environment where even someone who knows very little about music and record buying feels comfortable enough to walk through the doors and spend some time.

These pillars of musical discovery become regular haunts for thousands of people, who find solace in their four walls, meeting fellow vinyl enthusiasts, uncovering a whole world of music they'd never known before, and even befriending the shop owners (which can lead to getting first dibs on the best records). Many of the best-known stores in the world have stood the test of time, weathering the global dip in record sales during the 1990s and early 2000s and enjoying the recent renaissance that has put vinyl back on the map.

The feeling you get when perusing the shelves of record shops is incredible— from the aroma of old acetate and the anticipation when on the hunt for a specific record to the buzz of the store itself and the physical act of flicking through shelf after shelf of records. It's a well-trodden path, with millions of enthusiasts all over the planet working tirelessly to boost their collections and track down some of the more elusive rare cuts that are said to be out there (including a fair few fabled cuts that no one ever seems to be able to find).

This book is a guide to some of the planet's very best record shops, which epitomize the vinyl outlet of the 21st century—from Kenya to Colombia, Australia to Canada, these are 80 of the finest. So, join us as we go *Around the World in 80 Record Stores*...

INTRODUCTION

TOKYO · HC-R
RED EYE RECORDS · SYDNEY
MAZEEKA SAMIR FOUAD · CAIRO
NEW GRAMOPHONE HOUSE · NEW DELHI
Eureka Records · Buenos Aires
PICCADILLY RECORDS · MANCHESTER · PR-1978
HAPPYFEET · PRAGUE · SFR 2009
Superfly Records · PARIS · SFR 2009
Honest Jon's · LONDON · London · HJO-1974
THE CRYPT OF THE WIZARD · TCOTW-2017 · LONDON · SFR 2009

ABOVE
Honest Jon's,
London

Chapter One

United Kingdom

BELOW
Staff at Piccadilly Records, Manchester

Honest Jon's | London

What?	**Dub techno to modern jazz**
Where?	**278 Portobello Road, London W10 5TE**
When?	**1974**
Why?	**If those record shelves could speak…**

Over 40 years in the business means Honest Jon's holds a hell of a lot of history in its walls. Its standing within the London record-buying scene, as well as its global reputation, is thanks to several key elements: the number of influential figures who have passed through its doors, the musical knowledge of the owners, the quality of the records it stocks, and its contribution to music culture, period. It is an iconic record shop blessed with an impeccable rep.

The atmosphere has always been friendly and inclusive, with the local area a melting pot of cultures and ethnicities since the mid-20th century. As a result, the store's clientele has been a kaleidoscopic mix of color from day one. In particular, west London's Afro-Caribbean community has been intrinsic to Honest Jon's growth and the musical education of its owner, John (formerly known as Jon) Clare. He took over the shop in 1974 after the previous owner, his friend Jeff Francis, moved on to another vinyl retailer.

Amusingly, the premises had been a butcher's prior to Francis taking it over in those early days and he hadn't done much to change the interior, displaying records on the marble slabs once used to showcase meat, and the floors were apparently still bloodstained. This location, at 76 Golborne Road, was where the first incarnation of Honest Jon's stood for five years before

it moved down the road to its current home. In the late 1970s, John and his ex-business partner Dave Ryner opened a few other shops across London: one in Camden, one on Oxford Street, two in Soho, and one in Chelsea. However, by 1982 all the locations they'd set up were closed; Ryner took charge of the Camden store (changing the name to Rhythm Records) and John went back to focusing on numero uno, the original Honest Jon's in west London.

LEFT
Soul and Funk, just two of the many genres stocked at Honest Jon's.

UNITED KINGDOM

ABOVE
While the area around Honest Jon's has changed beyond recognition, the high quailty of music offered in store remains constant.

More than a mere shop, Honest Jon's has been an important cultural hub ever since it first popped up. Artists such as John Lydon, Joe Strummer, and Courtney Pine are long-time customers, while former employees include influential figures such as James Lavelle, the man behind Mo' Wax, and Anthony Wood, founder of *The Wire* magazine. In short, Honest Jon's is a legendary place that has not only supplied the best reggae, ska, jazz, soul, RnB, and electronic music for over 40 years, but also been intrinsic to the growth of the British music scene, in turn influencing the global music sphere.

HMV | London

What?	**Pop, rock, commercial music**
Where?	**363 Oxford Street, London W1C 2LA**
When?	**1921**
Why?	**One of the world's most iconic record shops**

In 1921 The Gramophone Company, one of the earliest recording enterprises in the UK, launched the first HMV store on Oxford Street in the center of London, a destination that has been satisfying the needs of record junkies for generations since.

HMV, or His Master's Voice, is named after a painting by Francis Barraud of a dog listening to a gramophone. The picture was purchased by The Gramophone Company in 1899, becoming the shop's logo when it opened 22 years later. The famous logo, featuring the silhouette of Nipper the dog and a gramophone, adorns the huge space above the shop's entrance, in bright neon lighting—an iconic image familiar to record collectors from every corner of the planet.

The history of the iconic Oxford Street location is entwined with that of London itself. During World War II, the basement was used as an official air-raid shelter, when hundreds of Londoners hid under the vinyl shelves to protect themselves from the bombs that were dropping outside. Another claim to fame is that Brian Epstein, manager of The Beatles, used the shop's recording facilities to cut a demo by the band before they were signed. According to the legend, the tracks were heard by publishing company Ardmore & Beechwood, based at the very same address, who linked Epstein up with record producer George Martin, then working at Parlophone. Had it not been for that fateful connection, The Beatles may never have been signed and become global superstars.

In the time since that very first branch was opened, the brand has been through an incredible journey, peaking in the 1990s with 320 stores across Great Britain and the rest of the world. It took a few decades for HMV to start to really expand, and it wasn't until 1966 that the high street brand capitalized on its success and grew in stature. Its presence was felt in most cities and towns around England, Scotland, Wales and the rest of Britain throughout the 1960s and '70s. In those two decades HMV achieved the accolade of Britain's biggest music retailer. In 1986 the company opened its huge flagship store further down Oxford Street. Whereas the original location opening was attended by famous British composer Sir Edward William Elgar, the '80s launch saw appearances from late INXS frontman Michael Hutchence and Sir Bob Geldof.

During the early 2000s, the global decline in record sales and physical purchases presented its challenges to HMV. However, the company has managed to weather the storm, diversifying its output to ensure it is ever-present on the UK high street. HMV still brings in huge acts like Ed Sheeran and Metallica for in-store performances, using their clout to boost their credentials and remind the record-buying public that they are still a major player. The original Oxford Street branch remains one of the chain's most popular stores with its iconic sign, history, and an extensive stock dedicated to all things pop culture. The shop floor is lined with racks of CDs and vinyl, plus merchandise from a wide range of pop stars and bands, plus thousands of videogames and movies. As a global brand that has captured the imaginations of millions of music lovers since it was first conceived, HMV is an untouchable force and a legendary record outlet.

BELOW
In 2021 HMV will celebrate its 100th year on London's Oxford Street, Europe's busiest shopping street.

Crypt of the Wizard | London

What?	**Heavy metal**
Where?	**324C Hackney Road, London E2 7AX**
When?	**2017**
Why?	**For a midweek mosh**

Heavy metal is a style of music that will never lose its potency, ever. The popularity of metal bands remains high despite what you may see in the charts and hear on the radio. Metal fans are diehards and they are just as dedicated to collecting their favorite bands' music as they are about everything else. You name it: hoodies, T-shirts, sweatshirts, beanie hats, socks, sweatbands, and much more, the fans lap it all up. So, to have a record shop dedicated to a genre with such committed fans, old and young, is akin to creating an oasis in the desert. It is a much-needed haven for those who love the dark and furious energy of heavy metal.

As you might expect, the interior of Crypt of the Wizard is shadowy and stacked with around 1,000-plus records, the majority of which are adorned with the kind of gothic artwork—pentagrams, images of demons, medieval fonts, blood, and skulls, and everything else you can think of—that's associated with the dark side of life. The guys behind it, Charlie Wooley (manager) and Marcus Mustafa (owner), are both fiends for the music, christening the store as a nod to rock band Mortiis and the compilation they put out in 1996. Though it's a relatively young shop, compared with others in London, Crypt of the Wizard has an established feel, as though it's been on the Hackney Road for a few decades. The vibe is sociable, and the team of staff is second to none when it comes to their knowledge of both the history of the music and what's happening now. You can also find a ton of heavy-metal magazines, as well as flyers for local and national events, plus a good selection of merch.

ABOVE
"Heavy Metal Record Shop." Crypt of the Wizard does what it says on the T-shirt.

Alan's Record & CD Shop | London

What?	**Secondhand records**
Where?	**218 High Road, East Finchley, London N2 9AY**
When?	**1994**
Why?	**Old-school, DIY, record-shop atmosphere at its best**

Simplicity is the key selling point of Alan's Record & CD Shop in north London. This is a proper record store: no gimmicks, no frills, just a great selection of secondhand vinyl of all kinds, from old-school 78s to contemporary albums. Still, though it's relatively small, there are around 15,000 records to choose from and a further 3,500 CDs, if that's your bag. The beauty of this little place is not just the location—way off the beaten path in a relatively quiet part of the city—but also the fact that Alan himself is such a genuinely lovely person whose passion for music fills his shop with positive ions. The atmosphere is chilled, welcoming, and intimate; you can browse anonymously if you like or spend a few hours chatting with Alan or other collectors. This is a store that really upholds the traditions of record buying effortlessly because it is what it is and isn't trying to be anything else. Apparently, some of the regular customers have Alan's personal number and vice versa, with the main man calling them if he comes across anything he thinks they'll like. Now that's what you call personal service.

ABOVE
Small but perfectly formed, Alan's manages to cram an incredible amount of music between its four walls.

Kristina Records | London

What?	**An eclectic selection of music, new and secondhand**
Where?	**44 Stoke Newington Road, London N16 7XJ**
When?	**2011**
Why?	**Cool, intimate, east London vibes**

Named after a "special someone," Kristina Records opened in 2011 in Dalston, a flagship area for gentrification in London. It's thanks in part to the growth of the area—which has been fueled by the migration of creatives, students, and young professionals—that the shop was able to open and become an immediate success. All three men who conceived Kristina Records were employees at the same record store before deciding to get together and launch their own little vinyl boutique—646 square feet (60 square meters) of it to be precise.

Owners Jack Rollo, Jason Spinks, and James Thorington spent almost a decade between them working at Notting Hill's Music & Video Exchange, their combined knowledge and experience giving birth to Kristina in all its minimal splendor. This is a contemporary space, where the design and overall aesthetic have been carefully considered, resulting in the immaculate, ordered feel of the interior. Designers Arris London took the site of a former real-estate office and transformed it into a space that exudes Scandinavian elegance, all cobalt-blue and exposed concrete. It's a great space to display the records, which benefit from an almost obsessive-compulsive categorization.

Jack, James, and Jason take their stock from distributors, people who pop in with secondhand records to sell, and people who want to donate their collections. So dedicated are they to providing the best possible service that they actually offer to visit the homes of potential donors so they can sift through their collections and work out if they're right for the store. Kristina's location is spot on, too—on Stoke Newington Road, at the top end of Dalston's main high street surrounded by Turkish newsagents and restaurants, clubs like The Nest and Birthdays, and an array of other cafés and local enterprises. Kristina Records has become part of the local community and welcomes visitors from all over the world on a weekly basis, thus becoming part of the global record-shop community in the process.

Sounds of the Universe | London

What?	Disco, funk, soul, jazz, electronic, reggae, African beats, all that good stuff
Where?	7 Broadwick Street, Soho, London W1F 0DA
When?	1992
Why?	For a true taste of international music

Starting life as a stall in Camden means Sounds of the Universe has humble roots, and you can feel that as soon as you walk into its Soho incarnation. There's a very rootsy, earthy feel to the place, as if you've been welcomed into owner Stuart Baker's private stash. You feel immediately at home, and that comforting atmosphere means you'll end up perusing the shelves for hours without ever checking the time, a rare feeling for most of the world's population in this day and age.

For musical discovery and investigation there aren't many places within a 10-mile (16-km) radius that compare to Sounds of the Universe, with its stock of international music ranging from Brazilian funk and jazz to Middle Eastern productions, and, of course, a healthy selection of UK and US soul, RnB, alt-rock, and much more. It's almost certain that you will discover something new when you pay a visit, and that's just upstairs where all the new releases are. Down in the secondhand basement is another treasure trove of "black gold," as some people like to call it— rows and rows of enchanting vinyl, lovingly displayed for the purpose of being rehomed and given a new lease of life.

Sounds of the Universe is closely tied in with the Soul Jazz Records label, which Stuart also set up in 1992. Soul Jazz reps a variety of music, reflecting the eclectic policy of its sister store, and has picked up a solid reputation in the years since it launched that feeds back into the shop. Customers at Sounds of the Universe can also sift through tons of CDs and a plethora of books and films, too. One of its claims to fame is that The Rolling Stones had one of their first ever rehearsals upstairs, when the building was a pub called The Bricklayers Arms. Keith Richards mentions it in his autobiography, saying that it all began around May 1962. So there's an air of musical history permeating the building's structure; combine that with a sterling music selection and the multicultural nature of Soho itself, and you've got a winning formula that has created one of London's premier record stores.

ABOVE
Given the label and the shop are run by the same people, Soul Jazz Records feature prominently in store.

Phonica Records | London

What?	**Electronic music of many varieties**
Where?	**51 Poland Street, Soho, London W1F 7LZ**
When?	**2003**
Why?	**Excellent curation for true heads**

Soho was once London's record-shop hub, with outlets seemingly on every street of the once-edgy district. In the 21st century, though, many of the great stores fell foul of changes to the area: increased rent and new developments (such as Crossrail) have led to the demise of several key places. However, there are some survivors and Phonica Records is one of them. Though the store is still quite young, it has a sterling rep among avid record buyers and industry heads alike. This is mainly thanks to the hard work put in by its three founders: Simon Rigg, Heidi Van Den Amstel (aka DJ Heidi), and Tom Relleen—each of the trio injected a lifetime of positive energy into building the foundations of what has become the Phonica of today.

Somehow, without advertising and launching at a time when other shops were closing, they managed to establish their store among London's record-buying community, with tons of DJs among their growing fanbase in those early days. Though they represented a wide range of club music and electronica, one particular sound was resonating at the time and helped catapult Phonica into the consciousness of electronic music consumers. It was the sound inspired by German techno label Kompakt, a style that popped up a few years before the minimal explosion of the mid-2000s—as Phonica was one of the few locations that sold records of this nature, they found favor with fans and were quickly established as the go-to spot for that style of music.

Over the years Phonica has employed several people who have gone on to enjoy successful DJ careers, most notably one of the founders, Heidi, who became a Radio 1 host.

LEFT
Expect to find promos and white labels from cutting-edge electronic music labels.

Heidi also tours the globe and set up her own party brand and label, Jackathon. Will Saul, who runs Aus Records, also worked at the store, as did techno selectors Anthea and Hector. In fact, of all the places in this book, Phonica has probably employed more international stars than any other.

Inside the shop you'll find well-organized rows of records for sale, as well as those displayed behind the counter—new, old, test presses, and special editions are all available—plus there are several listening points located at the main counter. The store has a communal atmosphere, often quite transient at weekends, perhaps a little quieter during the week. Expect to spy the odd famous face here and there, as many of the world's best-known house and techno DJs will pop in for a spot of digging when they're in town. Phonica has also become renowned for hosting in-store DJ sets, which always result in the shop being packed out, with music fans often spilling into the street, such is the popularity of these sessions. DJs such as Louie Vega, Ellen Allien, Nightmares On Wax, Tim Sweeney, Todd Edwards, Jacques Greene, Audion (aka Matthew Dear), Soulwax, and many more have graced the decks and caused a roadblock on Poland Street. Nowadays Phonica continues to support the very best in house, techno, and a myriad related genres and subgenres, while attracting visitors from across London, the rest of the UK, and the world.

RIGHT
Pay a visit to Phonica and there's every chance you could be flicking through these racks next to some of the best underground dance music DJs in the world.

Rough Trade West | London

What?	**Underground to mainstream**
Where?	**130 Talbot Road, London W11 1JA**
When?	**1976**
Why?	**It's a British record-shop institution**

One of the best-known record shops in London, and the rest of the world, too, Rough Trade has been in operation for over 40 years and can be found in both east and west London. The very first Rough Trade shop was the west London outlet, which was set up in February 1976 by Geoff Travis who, up until that point, was a drama teacher. The success of his first record-selling enterprise took him from the education system into the music industry and two years after the launch of the vinyl stockist he got Rough Trade Records off the ground, becoming a label boss in the process. The label picked up a little-known band called The Smiths in 1983, which helped to put Rough Trade Records on the map. Since then they have signed music from an exhaustive list of highly-regarded acts including Arcade Fire, The Strokes, British Sea Power, Mystery Jets, Belle & Sebastian, and many many more. A smaller offshoot was opened in Covent Garden in 1988, and traded until 2007 just before their flagship east London outpost was launched in Brick Lane. Over the years they have also had stores open and close in Tokyo, Paris, and San Francisco plus two other UK outlets in Nottingham and Bristol, plus one across the Atlantic in New York (the city's biggest record shop).

Rough Trade stocks an eclectic range of sounds, from chart music and indie to underground dance music, leftfield electronica, and sci-fi soundtracks. The west London shop itself is everything you'd expect from a record shop, well-organised, the walls plastered with posters, and full of keen music enthusiasts from all walks of life. Heavenly.

LEFT
Geoff Travis back in the early days of Rough Trade.

ABOVE
Customers browse the racks at Rough Trade West. Be sure to head east to their second store, just off London's Brick Lane.

Spillers Records | Cardiff

What?	**A bit of everything**
Where?	**27 Morgan Arcade, Cardiff CF10 1AF**
When?	**1894**
Why?	**It's the oldest record store in the world!**

Spillers Records, in Cardiff, has quite a claim to fame, being touted as "the oldest record store in the world." Established in 1894, it has been around for well over 120 years which is an impressive feat, whether it really is the oldest record shop in the world or not. Henry Spiller opened the store in Queen's Arcade all those years ago, specializing in gramophones, shellac discs, and wax phonograph cylinders and mostly intending to cater for aspiring coal merchants who were accumulating wealth through the export of the fossil fuel. Seeing an opportunity to capitalize on the new technology and the boost in his city's local economy, he opened Spillers and it remains one of Cardiff's prized record shops over a century later. He passed the store on to his son Edward in the early 1920s, who added musical instruments to Spillers' repertoire and was joined by popular musician Joe Gregory—who was a wizard on the accordion.

Of course, being around for so long means that there's been the odd period of drama, including several changes of location, being sold on due to family disputes, surviving the impact of the Internet on physical sales, and threats of closure. The shop has weathered every storm, though, and is currently owned by Ashli Todd, the daughter of former owner Nick Todd who took over managerial duties at Spillers back in 1975. Nick was a regular customer and, during one of his visits, the former manageress told him she'd had enough and asked if he wanted her job. Eleven years later, he bought the store.

At the height of Spillers' popularity back in the 1980s and 1990s, there would be queues of people snaking from the inside of the shop out into the street, as eager collectors and music fans waited to get a chance to pop inside and grab the latest releases or dig for rarities. Inside the bright, glass-fronted store are neat rows of records and CDs, all sold at competitive prices by staff members who know their stuff and are more than happy to share their expertise with anyone wishing to pick their brains. From hip hop to psych rock, soundtracks and goth, it's all there and the atmosphere couldn't be any more warm and welcoming.

RIGHT
If a record shop can exist for well over 100 years, it must be doing something right. In the case of Spillers they are doing a lot of things right.

Idle Hands | Bristol

What?	**From house, techno, and disco to reggae, dubstep, grime, and dub**
Where?	**32a City Road, Bristol BS2 8TP**
When?	**2011**
Why?	**For a taster of Bristol's ever-fertile music scene**

There must be something in the River Avon's water because Bristol never seems to have a let-up in its constant flow of music and talented new artists—from Massive Attack to more recent heroes such as dubstep innovators Joker and Pinch; house heads like Julio Bashmore and Eats Everything; and, of course, the mighty Roni Size, Krust, Tricky, Portishead, and many more. The scene is always buzzing, and Idle Hands sits comfortably as a key destination among the city's fertile community of musicians and artists. Launched as the offshoot of a record label by Chris Farrell (who ran Rooted Records with Peverelist), it's a friendly, cozy place with a modern interior and lovely staff.

Originally located in Stokes Croft, the store moved to its new premises on City Road in St. Paul's at the beginning of 2017. It's a great spot, very close to the center of Bristol and in a multicultural area that is a great mix of locals, students, and young professionals, all of whom give the district its unique character. Bristol itself is renowned for its laid-back outlook, "the mild, mild west" as it says on a painting by local hero Banksy—as a result, you can expect a similar feeling at Idle Hands. No intimidating looks of scorn from wizened old record collectors there, just the kind of gentle charm you can only find in Bristol.

RIGHT
If you want to hear the latest underground sounds coming out of Bristol, head here.

UNITED KINGDOM

Piccadilly Records | Manchester

What?	**Across the board, from Balearic and disco to rock and indie**
Where?	**53 Oldham Street, Manchester M1 1JR**
When?	**1978**
Why?	**Diversity and professionalism**

Over four decades in the game and millions of satisfied customers later, Piccadilly Records is a pillar of the Manchester music scene. Vinyl collectors can be very particular and, as a result, rather critical, both of music and the shops that sell it— so it's a testament to Piccadilly's professionalism that it has virtually no bad reviews online. In fact, many people have taken the time to give extensive feedback on the store, demonstrating how much of a positive effect it has had on the public.

It was in the post-punk era that the shop really came into its own, stocking a variety of rock, indie, pop, and alternative music and flourishing to become a part of the city's musical fabric. The eclectic selection of music they sell means the clientele is equally varied, from young music fans who want to pick up some contemporary pop—or concert tickets—to older collectors who are hoping to snag a rare secondhand catch of the day, or perhaps a special edition reissue. It's all there under one roof, with music in both vinyl and CD formats. Rows and rows of carefully organized and labeled record shelves greet you when you walk in from Oldham Street; the atmosphere is about as friendly as you can imagine—particularly as the store is in Manchester, which is one of the most down-to-earth cities in the UK. If you've never experienced northern charm before, you can expect a large dollop of it there.

Current owners Laura Kennedy, Philippa Jarman, and Darryl Mottershead took over the shop in 1990 and relocated from the original location to Manchester's lively Northern Quarter in 1997. A key area of renewal in the city center, the Northern Quarter has become increasingly popular over the last couple of decades and Piccadilly Records owes some of its prosperity to being in such a great location. At the core of this success, though, is the diverse selection of music they stock and the friendly, knowledgeable staff. Working at the counter of a record shop where the styles on offer are so varied is no mean feat, so you know you're in good hands if the person serving you is able to confidently segue from musing on the finer points of Joy Division's early work into a full and frank dissection of Katy Perry's new single.

ABOVE
A town with as rich a musical history as Manchester
deserves a top record store. Piccadilly delivers in spades.

Rubadub Records | Glasgow

What?	**Finest quality electronic music**
Where?	**35 Howard Street, Glasgow G1 4BA**
When?	**1992**
Why?	**To experience a cornerstone of the UK techno scene**

Martin McKay opened the doors of the mighty Rubadub Records in Glasgow on August 10, 1992. Along with Alan Gray and, a few months later, Wilba Sandieson, McKay got Rubadub going with £1,000 and not much else, apart from a set of decks and an idea to get a record store off the ground. Techno formed the foundation of the music policy there, and it remains one of the most important techno outlets in the UK, with a distribution wing that supports a wide range of independent labels and artists. In the early days, strong connections with Detroit and Chicago helped them to stock up on a plethora of hot new releases from some of the most influential labels in the 1990s, including Transmat, Plus8, and Underground Resistance, among others.

Rubadub's position within Glasgow's highly respected techno scene was cemented very early on in the shop's lifetime when a local curry house opened up its basement as a rave space, inviting the Rubadub crew to host parties there. Club 69 became a legendary spot, with a sea of intrepid, Glaswegian techno-explorers making their way out of the city every week to attend the sweaty basement. Its original location was in Paisley, 20 minutes west of Glasgow's center, though it moved to its current home on Howard Street in 1999 after the second store had to be closed when the Virginia Galleries (where it was housed) suffered huge subsidence due to underground construction work taking place nearby. After a difficult six-month spell in a temporary space, McKay and Sandieson were able to use their insurance payout to relocate to their current address.

The courteous staff at Rubadub Records are all music aficionados themselves—making it, playing it, collecting it, and living for it, which means their insider knowledge is second to none. The latest incarnation of Rubadub also stocks a wide range of music technology, and production and performance equipment, giving it a far wider scope than places that only sell records. Again, the staff are able to offer expert insight into all the gear they sell, which makes shopping at Rubadub a dream for anyone who steps through the door. Former employees include Jackmaster, Denis Sulta, and Spencer, all young bucks who were nurtured and mentored by the Rubadub team. With all that in mind, it's easy to see why the shop is so intrinsic to Glasgow's electronic music scene.

Unknown Pleasures | Edinburgh

What?	New wave and prog rock through to old-school hip hop
Where?	110 Canongate, Old Town, Edinburgh EH8 8DD
When?	2006
Why?	Unusual selection of music and merch, plus exemplary service

A spot that shares the same name as the classic album by Joy Division must be pretty good, right? Of course, there's a lot more to this Edinburgh-based outlet than its name alone, but it's a definite seal of quality that precedes your visit. Inside the store is a top-notch selection of vinyl, mostly secondhand, ranging from new wave and punk to old-school hip hop. The shop's owners have curated a wonderful collection of music and seem to be able to snag the kind of rare or forgotten-about releases that you only remember once you come face to face with them. So, a friendly warning here, you may end up leaving with a lot more than you bargained for. This is the beauty of record shopping: you go out looking for one thing and come back with 20 others that you never even thought you'd pick up, and Unknown Pleasures seems to be able to cultivate that kind of situation time and again.

ABOVE
You can't visit Edinburgh without a walk down the Royal Mile, which means you can't miss the opportunity to walk into Unknown Pleasures.

The location is pretty small, but its intimate interior only adds to the personal experience you get when you're there. Its position, at the end of the Royal Mile, is perfect— central enough to make it convenient to get to and an attractive prospect to passersby. The company that runs Unknown Pleasures, Vinylnet, also owns a shop in Manchester, so you can be sure they know what they're doing. Everything seems to be done with authenticity; there's no pretence or a need to be seen as "cool" or "trendy"—just that all-important and genuine love of collecting and sharing music. It's the glue that binds all music-lovers and record stores together. Make sure you're ready for a good old dig, with a credit card at the ready, because Unknown Pleasures is a goldmine of secondhand vinyl and you will be enchanted by the rows and rows of mint-condition music they stock.

UNITED KINGDOM

ABOVE Wally's Groove World, Antwerp

Chapter Two

Europe

2

Flur Discos | Lisbon

What?	**Everything you can imagine and lots more**
Where?	**Avenida Infante D. Henrique, Armazém B4 Cais da Pedra, Santa Apolónia, 1900 Lisbon, Portugal**
When?	**2001**
Why?	**A direct line to what's happening in the Lisbon underground**

This neat little space is right next to Lisbon's River Tagus, so it's perfect for post-digging, waterfront, chill-out vibes. Opened in 2001 by José Moura and Pedro Santos, the size of the store belies its hefty and incredibly diverse collection of sounds from all over the world and from almost every genre you can think of (and probably a few you've never heard of). Due to its extensive and eclectic selection, Flur Discos has become an essential destination for eager diggers from all over planet Earth, many of whom will spend hours trawling through the seemingly endless racks of vinyl lining the walls of the shop's long, narrow interior.

Lisbon is one of Europe's most abundant cultural centers, and Flur Discos represents its musical heritage to the fullest; with a considerable collection of Portuguese music, some of it represents the ghost of Lisbon's past, but the majority is comprised of brand-new material from the city's ever-growing community of musicians and independent labels. In fact, José himself co-runs a label focused on supporting electronic music produced by Lisbon's huge pool of talent. The label, Principe Discos, pushes a very unique sound that is peculiar to Lisbon, think African influences spliced with house and techno tropes. You'll find a healthy selection of this kind of style at Flur Discos, in among the krautrock, jazz, soul, heavy metal, and countless other genres.

ABOVE
Flur Discos offers up an excellent cross-section of what fuels the Lisbon music scene.

In-store DJ sets are not uncommon; local selectors are often on the bill, with international heroes also popping in from time to time—the mighty Gilles Peterson is one of many legends to have spun on the decks. There are also the standard "listening spots" (i.e. a pair of Technics 1210s), so you can spend a while skipping through the pile of records you've scooped up from the shelves. The atmosphere is lively and sociable, and a warmth pervades the store which makes you feel instantly at home. This is a real haven for vinyl enthusiasts and the location is unbeatable; there really isn't much that compares to examining your brand-new vinyl purchases while the sun glistens off the River Tagus on a hot summer's day.

ABOVE
In recent years Lisbon has earned itself a reputation as one of Europe's coolest cities to visit, helped in no small part by places like Flur Discos.

Discos Paradiso | Barcelona

What?	**Electronic through to psych rock**
Where?	**Carrer de Ferlandina 39, 08001 Barcelona, Spain**
When?	**2010**
Why?	**That sound system...**

Barcelona has long been established as a center for arts, culture, and music, so it's no surprise that it's home to Discos Paradiso—a marvelous place right in the middle of El Raval, Barcelona's most vibrant and colorful neighborhood. The store was opened in 2010 and has quickly become a go-to spot for the city's record-collecting community, as well as diggers from all over the world. The guys behind Discos Paradiso, Arnau Farrés and Gerard Condemines, are your archetypal record-store owners—both have a deep passion for collecting records and their small, yet perfectly formed, shop is the natural progression of both men's lifelong fascination with vinyl.

Though the focus is on electronic music, the range of other genres on sale there is vast, from psychedelic rock through to contemporary techno and house, and the quality is high across the board. Besides its ample stock of new releases, Discos Paradiso also has an impressive amount of secondhand records on its shelves, which is always good, especially for those who want to hunt down those rare gems that often crop up when someone kindly donates their old assortment of records.

The shop itself is petite and the decor minimal, showcasing the records and the music-playing equipment in a clean, white space that almost feels like a small art gallery. In fact, one of the walls is used as an "exhibition" space of sorts, with a collage of Polaroids featuring some of the store's most famous visitors and many of their customers, too. International DJs and musicians often pop by when they're in town to riffle through the racks and chat with the owners—famous faces who've passed through the doors include Ben UFO, the mighty KRS-One, Mike Huckaby, Jeremy Underground Paris, and many, many more. If that wasn't enough, Arnau and Gerard regularly organize in-store gigs and DJ sets, which are hugely popular. Avid fans will be seen forming a scrum outside the shop's doors as they vie for a good position to see whoever is playing. They also launched their own record label (Urpa I Musell) in late 2017 with a reissue of the superb LP *Ambientes Hormonales* by El Sueño De Hyparco, which originally hit the shelves in 1990.

Now firmly rooted in the city's highly fertile music scene, Discos Paradiso is an essential stop-off for anyone who wants to pick up a wide range of electronica and lots more. Make sure you check out their superb sound system as well; it's an absolute peach.

EUROPE

RIGHT
Cutting-edge records played through
crystal-clear speakers. Welcome to Paradiso.

Superfly Records | Paris

What?	**Rare cuts and represses from around the globe**
Where?	**53 Rue Notre Dame de Nazareth, 75003 Paris, France**
When?	**2009**
Why?	**There is nowhere else like this in Paris**

Run by a team of dedicated diggers, Superfly Records specializes in collectibles, rare finds, and a treasury of secondhand gold. Paulo Goncalves and Manu Boubli are the captains of the good ship Superfly, and their mission is to deliver a plethora of the good stuff from the world's finest music makers. It's one of those spots that has achieved cult status, thanks to a singular vision, and you won't find anywhere similar in Paris. Superfly came into being fairly recently in 2009, but what it lacks in its own history it more than makes up for with the history of some of the records it sells. Shopping in Superfly is like jumping into a time machine that takes you back to bygone eras in parts of the planet that most of the commercial music industry rarely thinks about: Africa, South America, and the Far East all feature in their extensive collection. You won't just find indigenous sounds from those territories, but also a wide variety of genres you may not expect. Japanese jazz, African disco and funk, rare Latin pressings, odd South American represses, and a mindboggling list of other such "niche" styles are stocked at Superfly.

The shop itself is quite petite, but provides enough space for you to feel at ease, even when it's crowded, thanks to the thoughtful design and layout. As keen collectors themselves, all the guys who work at Superfly can't help but enthuse about the music and will happily devote themselves to assisting you. As most record-store staff will tell you, it's pretty much a dream job and being able to share their knowledge and passion is one of the main factors behind this feeling of "living the dream." You'll feel that spirited vibe as soon as you approach the Superfly staff at the counter, so don't be afraid to ask for advice if you need it.

Paris is a multicultural city and Superfly is a great representation of the kaleidoscope of color that makes up the city's population, stretching out beyond the store to also include a record label. Taking the same approach as the shop, on Superfly Records you'll find a mouthwatering array of global sounds, all carefully curated by two men who are driven by an innate desire to share their love for music from all over the world.

ABOVE
Once you step foot in Superfly, be prepared to encounter some sublime releases in one of Paris' best record stores.

Syncrophone | Paris

What?	**House, techno, disco, and much more**
Where?	**6 Rue des Taillandiers, 75011 Paris, France**
When?	**2007**
Why?	**An electronic music powerhouse**

When it comes to house and techno, there aren't many places in Paris that can compete with Syncrophone. Not only is it a respected vinyl outlet with strong ties to many of the best-known heroes on the Paris underground, but it is also a long-running label and distributor, making the brand a formidable force. In 2005 Syncrophone was established within French music company Cyber Production by Blaise, Didier Allyne, and John Sill. All three men are stalwarts of the Paris scene, with their combined histories including successful DJ careers, event promotion, and, most importantly, working at record stores. John's experience came through a stint at Vibe Station, while Didier launched Trafic Records in 1998. Syncrophone went independent in 2007, moving away from Cyber Production when the shop opened, and they haven't looked back since. Nowadays they carry a huge stock of contemporary house and techno, plus hip hop, soul, and a bunch of other genres, some of which is released by the labels they represent and distribute—over 60 in total. The rest comes from the crème de la crème of underground electronic music purveyors and labels that push high-quality music from all over the planet. A few hours spent in Syncrophone will almost certainly result in you leaving with a bagful of killer vinyl and a big smile on your face.

A policy of "first come, first served" means Syncrophone's supply of records is very inclusive. A rule of keeping exclusives and white labels under the counter for certain DJs doesn't exist here—the team aims to give people what they want, hence the store's broad range of music and that progressive approach to stock. It makes Syncrophone a great place to visit because there's no secret hierarchy; everyone has an equal chance of finding that hot new record or a sought-after repress.

Friends of the shop include French trio Apollonia (check out their in-store DJ set from 2014 on YouTube), so don't be surprised if you bump into Dan Ghenacia from the supergroup, or any other well-known selectors from the French capital—or, in fact, any international visitors, since the store is a popular choice for DJs who are in town for the weekend. Outside the shop, label, and distribution business, there are also Syncrophone label nights, held at Badaboum (which is on the same street as the store). Fred P, Joey Anderson, and DJ QU are among the underground names who've appeared at their parties. The Syncrophone gang have also hosted several shows on Rinse FM France and DJ across the city and the rest of France. All the hard work that goes into this premier record shop is clear to see; you feel it as soon you step inside. Be sure to pay them a visit when you're in town.

ABOVE AND LEFT
The store has a simple layout designed to make the digging experience enjoyable and relaxed.

EUROPE

Radiation Records | Rome

What?	**Punk, rock, hardcore, and an eclectic selection of treats**
Where?	**Circonvallazione Casilina 44, 00176 Rome, Italy**
When?	**2005**
Why?	**Exceptional secondhand vinyl in one of Rome's most vibrant areas**

There are several boxes that need to be ticked for a record shop to rise above the competition and be regarded as one of the best. Radiation Records, of course, ticks them all, hence its appearance in this book. One of its key attributes is its location in Pigneto, which is regarded as one of Rome's most "hip" areas, with lots of fancy shops and restaurants. However, it's not too posh either, having quite a youthful zest. Being entrenched in such a buzzing hub of activity gives Radiation a good dose of positive energy; combine that with the enthusiasm of owner Marco Sannino and you've got a winning formula.

Marco opened the store in 2005, but he'd already been working in the vinyl distribution business for over a decade. He moved to Rome from Palermo, Sicily, in the early 1990s and got himself a job with Goodfellas, an outfit which was the main distributor of independent Italian music. Goodfellas had their own little spot, which stocked all the releases they were responsible for distributing. Marco's big break came when the shop moved to a bigger location and things didn't quite work out—he bought the premises and renamed the store Radiation Records, opening in December 2005. Secondhand vinyl makes up around 70 percent of the records on sale and, though you can find a wide range of musical styles, punk and hardcore are Marco's specialty. He plays in a band called ANTI YOU and also ran his own punk label called Gonna Puke back in the 1990s. The shop has two distinct sections: one room is dedicated to CDs and the other has an abundance of vinyl.

Radiation has a worldwide rep, and it's one of Rome's most important record stores, attracting customers, collectors, and vinyl tourists from all over Italy and the rest of the world. Marco and his staff members are all super-chilled, the kind of people who will gladly dedicate their time and energy to helping you with your enquiry, no matter how trivial it may seem. Overall this is one of the best vinyl outlets in Italy and more than worth a visit.

ABOVE
Radiation is able to satisfy your musical cravings seven days a week.

LEFT
As well as heaps of music, there are also plenty of interesting music-related books to browse.

EUROPE

Rollercoaster Records | Kilkenny

What?	**Americana, classic indie, and an assorted range of other delights**
Where?	**St. Kieran's Street, Kilkenny, Ireland**
When?	**2003**
Why?	**One of Ireland's best record stores and the happiest in the world!**

Rollercoaster Records calls itself "the happiest little record shop in the world," and for that reason alone it should be on your bucket list. Unfortunately, an air of sadness has been hanging over this brilliant Irish outlet since late 2017 when its owner, the legendary Willie Meighan, passed away less than a year after being diagnosed with terminal cancer. However, Rollercoaster Records continues to supply the very best in Americana, classic indie, and top-notch music from across the board, keeping Willie's memory and his optimistic attitude alive.

Records have been sold at the premises in Kilkenny since the late 1980s when it was known as Top Twenty. Willie started working there in 1990 and, 13 years later, he took over with his business partner Darragh Butler. Darragh's background as a drummer with rock band Kerbdog was perfectly suited to encourage the evolution of Top Twenty into Rollercoaster, while Willie's know-how helped take the shop to a whole new level. (Incidentally, Rollercoaster was the original name of Butler's band.) Willie's connection with the local music community and his interest in the ins and outs of the music business meant the store thrived and it grew in popularity, quickly acquiring a reputation across the globe.

At Rollercoaster you get the perfect balance of a welcoming atmosphere and the expertise of its employees, including manager Dave Holland. There's no chance of feeling intimidated there, or encountering a snobby clerk who makes you feel inferior. It isn't called "the happiest little record shop in the world" for no reason. The colorful interior features a lot of red fittings, shelves, and so on, to match the red in the shop's logo. It's small, but big enough to handle live performances—usually from solo artists or double acts—and occasionally ambitious enough to put on bands. Since Willie died the store has continued to trade, his wife now taking a more prominent role in the business. It's been a difficult time for all involved since he passed away, but there's no doubt that his memory is well and truly alive in everything they do, and for that all the team at Rollercoaster Records should be proud of themselves.

EUROPE

RIGHT
Rollercoaster is not just a local institution, but is treasured by music fans across Ireland for its excellent service and selection.

Doctor Vinyl | Brussels

What? **High-caliber electronica**

Where? **Rue de la Grande Ile 1, 1000 Brussels, Belgium**

When? **1997**

Why? **To experience a lynchpin of the Brussels' electronic music scene**

If you stand back and take a long, hard look at some of the world's best record shops, you'll see that one common characteristic is a unique, and usually highly influential: position within their city's music scene. Doctor Vinyl most definitely transcends its four cramped walls, with an influence that permeates the clubs and music studios of the Belgian capital to inspire its musicians and provide the foundation for a strong community. It all started in 1997 when the owner, and (of course) vinyl-obsessed DJ, Geert Sermon opened the now iconic spot in the Saint Géry district of Brussels, right next to the River Zenne. It's a great location in the heart of an area that's always buzzing with activity, especially at night, thanks to all the bars, clubs, and restaurants. This energy feeds back into Geert's store and it has become a hub for the city's DJs and electronic music enthusiasts. In fact, on any day of the week you are likely to encounter a very busy, buoyant store, full of chat, pumping music, and a variety of customers all hanging out and catching up on the latest music gossip. The vibe is laid back; even if you're not fussed about buying any records, you can always spend time chatting with Geert or any other customers who happen to be hanging out.

Doctor Vinyl has been at the epicenter of the Brussels' electronic music scene for over two decades now, and it has achieved legendary status thanks to its longevity and unerring commitment to providing the best new releases to its clientele, while proudly

ABOVE
Belgium has a thriving electronic music scene, and Doctor Vinyl will guide you to some of its finest protagonists.

LEFT
With over 20 years in the game, Doctor Vinyl has built up a loyal customer base of music lovers.

maintaining an ethos centered on community and socializing. One of Geert's proudest moments to date was being involved in the 2013 documentary The Sound Of Belgium, a film which traced the roots of the country's highly influential new beat movement. Geert provided the soundtrack and his status as a key member of his country's music scene was cemented with that legendary film. Meanwhile, Doctor Vinyl's standing was also reinforced, and it continues to maintain its position as one of Belgium's very best record outlets.

Music Mania | Ghent

What?	**Anything and everything you could want, and more**
Where?	**Sint-Pietersnieuwstraat 19, 9000 Ghent, Belgium**
When?	**1969**
Why?	**An historical and cultural beacon of the Belgian music scene**

Music Mania is one of Belgium's longest-serving record stores, making it an invaluable source of information and vinyl with significant historical and cultural influence. Its doors first opened way back in the magical summer of '69, a time when the world was going through a spiritual revolution and music was intrinsic to a lot of the changes taking place. Out of this revolutionary era Music Mania was born, and it quickly became a hub for Ghent's music aficionados, as well as anyone who happened to be visiting from out of town. Despite several internal overhauls and some changes of address over the past few decades, the core ethos of Music Mania has remained the same: to sell great music without prejudice. They have been staunchly maintaining this outlook for half a century, staying true to their beliefs and refusing to follow trends.

At Music Mania you'll find a wide variety of styles, from Belgian new beat and dark wave through to more contemporary techno releases, indie, funk, Afrobeat, and lots, lots more. What makes Music Mania so remarkable is the fact that it has a young team pulling the strings behind the scenes; this isn't an outlet that has become set in its ways or jaded. The core team—Lorin, Adriaan, and Karel—have been running things since 2008 and they make sure there is a fresh energy pulsating through the shop's walls, whether that be via all the new music they buy in, or the customers who pass through the doors. Another cornerstone of the store's appeal is readily given advice and freedom of information, so rest assured that you can ask staff members anything and they will be happy to assist. This has helped them become one of the most respected record outlets in Belgium, if not the world.

Music Mania is also responsible for two independent labels: Music Mania Records and Music Mania Reprise. The former focuses on unreleased Belgian work, while Reprise handles older releases, seeking out classic, often sought-after, and hard-to-get-hold-of records. In 2016 Music Mania co-launched STROOM Records, together with DJ Nosedrip, adding another outlet to their respected roster. The shop is bright and clean inside, with a considered, uncluttered layout—the corner location lets in a lot of light, so it feels more spacious than your average record store. The atmosphere can vary from quiet to buoyant depending on the day and the time of the week, but you'll always be warmly welcomed by the staff and you may even bump into a local musician or two. Legendary DJ duo 2ManyDJs are known to call the store home, so keep your eyes peeled, as well as your ears…

Wally's Groove World | Antwerp

What?	**Electronic, new and old**
Where?	**Lange Nieuwstraat 126, 2000 Antwerp, Belgium**
When?	**1997**
Why?	**A seminal Belgian record store**

When Koen van Immerseel (aka DJ Koenie) set up Wally's Groove World back in 1995, things were very different on planet Earth. Evolving in a world where online sales, streaming, and downloads (legal and illegal) have completely flipped the music industry on its head has been a challenge for Wally's, but it has remained a shining light in Belgium's busy student city, thanks to its dedication to the underground side of electronic music, whether it's straight from the old school or hot off the press.

Koenie's resumé includes working at USA Import, a highly influential record shop where his love for music of all kinds was solidified. In the era of Belgian new beat, USA Import was one of the most infamous stores and Koenie built his own reputation there, as well as keeping the store relevant and in tune with its customers' needs. Koenie's career went from strength to strength in that period, cementing his place in the Belgian music hall of fame way before Wally's Groove came into being. Of course, the knowledge he acquired at USA Import has been channeled into his own excellent location. Deep house to 90s acid-rave cuts are all there, neatly organized and arranged by category, with staff at hand to answer any questions.

ABOVE
With over 20 years in the game, Wally's remains a powerhouse within the Belgian underground.

There's a comforting ambience at Wally's—Koenie's own devotion to music permeates every aspect of the store and its simple, uncluttered layout allows the thousands of records to breathe, while also providing customers with a calm space in which to peruse the shelves.

One particularly cool feature is the technicolor wall, which adds a touch of character to the space. Another great addition is the in-store laptop on which you can search through the stock that's not on the shop floor. If you find what you're after, then staff members will happily go down into the basement and get it for you.

Like many of its counterparts worldwide, Wally's also has its own label wing, Wally's Groove World (WGW) Records, which is home to a wide variety of productions, from up-and-coming or slightly under-the-radar Belgian artists. This is Wally's true legacy; its support for local artists has been staunch from day one and if it wasn't for this iconic hub, a lot of Belgians wouldn't have had access to such a huge amount of great music. Famous faces pop in from time to time, Richie Hawtin among them—a co-sign from someone of Richie's caliber is always a bonus for a record store, being an indication that they're doing something right. From the basement to the shop floor and beyond, Wally's stands for quality electronic music.

CLONE | Rotterdam

What?	**Fresh electronic music**
Where?	**Raampoortstraat 12, 3032 AD Rotterdam, Netherlands**
When?	**1993**
Why?	**One of Rotterdam's longest standing electronic music outlets**

Launched as a techno label back in 1993, CLONE has grown into a veritable empire, with Serge Verschuur at the helm keeping it moving and evolving. Serge's down-to-earth ethos means CLONE is far from being your typical moody techno outfit, with staff and customers alike radiating warm, friendly vibes. The record-store branch of CLONE didn't come into being until the mid-1990s, two years after the label was born. Holland's music scene had become disparate, with commercial gabber and mainstream house dominating the landscape with not much else in between. Serge expanded the label activities and opened up a small shop in the back of a skate shop called Urban Unit, selling the same records to DJ friends and fellow collectors that would also sit happily in his own collection. With his uncompromising approach, Serge wanted to represent the "alternative" electronic music scene that only existed in the "underground," a counterpoint to the commercial dance scene which had taken over in the Lowlands at that time.

Having started very small at Urban Unit and working hard with an old-school mail-order service out of hours, CLONE soon developed a fan base all over the world. After moving to a different location in Rotterdam, de Nieuwe Binnenweg (known as the city's "music street," where nine other record stores were located at that time), CLONE was truly established as a specialist vinyl outlet, with customers from all over Holland, Belgium, and even Germany making regular pilgrimages to the store. The music policy was simple, kept to a very high level because Serge figured he could always keep anything that didn't sell and he didn't want to risk ending up with anything that was substandard. This outlook served him well, as the records began to sell,

ABOVE
Be sure to check out the new releases from CLONE's in-house label.

custom steadily increased, and CLONE was off to a strong start. Over the years it has achieved legendary status, and this is all down to Serge (who continues to collect avidly to this today) and his expanded team of expert staff with an unwavering passion for music. Serge's love for music of all kinds (which stems from a youth spent listening to and recording the radio) flows into the shop, where the stock is always fresh, whether it's hot from the pressing plant, releases from his own stable of CLONE sub-labels, or older cuts from around the globe.

The store itself no longer occupies a spot on de Nieuwe Binnenweg and can now be found in one of the arched passageways of the Hofbogen, just beneath former railway station Hofplein, where it houses over 15,000 records and the successful Clone.nl online store. It's a unique place with its arched ceiling and extraordinary length. This sets it apart from most record shops, which are either on the small side or humungous. Stepping into CLONE almost feels like stepping into Serge's own personal vinyl library— a space where you're allowed to peruse for as long as you like and where every single shelf and row of records has been lovingly cultivated and prepared by its proprietor.

Red Light Records | Amsterdam

What?	Electronic music that breaks the mold
Where?	Oudekerksplein 26, 1012 GZ Amsterdam, Netherlands
When?	2012
Why?	A record store that is unique and individual in every way

In Amsterdam, Red Light Records operates in the part of town most famous for its legal sex trade. Co-owners Abel Nagengast and James Pole helm the store, which first opened its doors back in 2012. The first thing you'll notice is that this exceptional spot is housed inside a room once used by a prostitute, retaining those infamous red lights—though now the only vice that can be indulged in there is a lust for unusual vinyl pressings. The exterior still features the typical kind of voyeuristic window you'll see all over the red-light district, and entry is only via a buzzer. This slightly subversive location means that a large percentage of those who enter the shop really want to be there; they've hunted it down, and made a bit of an effort to step into it. This filters out the droves of tourists that flood Amsterdam and its infamous district, leaving Red Light Records with only the most dedicated, discerning clientele. Perfect, since most of the music they stock is not geared toward a mass market. You could be mistaken for thinking that this is an elitist approach; however, this is most definitely not the case. Red Light Records is more of a specialist store than one that tries to be exclusive.

As soon as you step foot in this relaxed, friendly boutique, you will see how open and inclusive its staff members are. Ask them anything and they'll do their very best to help, often chipping in with useful recommendations, hints, or tips. They're very handy if you need to bounce some ideas around or just to find out about artists or labels similar to the ones you like. The music policy may well be slightly left-field, but it's important to remember that not everybody in the world listens to commercial music. In fact, it's refreshing to find somewhere that doesn't follow trends in order to assert its own identity and presents the record-buying public with something a little different from the norm. As you scan the shelves in the compact shop, you'll enter a whole other world of musical delights—from soul, funk, jazz, reggae, African, Brazilian, and krautrock to library sounds, ambient, electronica, TV and movie soundtracks, all the way up to disco, house, techno, and more.

Red Light Records is part of the Red Light Complex, a hub which includes a radio station and a record label, bringing together several platforms to form a powerhouse outfit that has become an intrinsic part of Amsterdam's highly productive electronic music community. Make sure you track them down and press that buzzer to enter another dimension in sound, illuminated by sleazy red lights.

Rush Hour | Amsterdam

What?	**House, techno, underground electronic**
Where?	**Spuistraat 116, 1012 VA Amsterdam, Netherlands**
When?	**1997**
Why?	**A legendary place that has pushed Amsterdam's music scene forward**

The Dutch have got it all sewn up, from their general outlook, healthy lifestyles, progressive attitudes to sex and drugs, forward-thinking education system, world-leading creative industries, and lots more. They seem to have it all, and their electronic music scene is one of the strongest in the world. From trance to techno, there is a never-ending list of Dutch artists who all put their own spin on their chosen genre with panache and dominate the world. All the while, the clubs and festivals keep the scene buoyant and invigorated, mostly with the support of the Government and local authorities. Record stores flourish in this kind of environment, and Rush Hour stands at the epicenter of Amsterdam's house and techno movement, delivering excellence in everything they do.

The shop launched in 1997, and has held its own ever since. Co-founder Antal Heitlager is a well-known face on Amsterdam's underground, super-connected with the city's labels, artists, and clubs, and a respected DJ talent in his own right. It's thanks to his leadership and the hard work of numerous Rush Hour family members that the store is still open and business is thriving. Inside you'll find a very stripped-back layout—no overfilled shelves or racks, just a very considered constellation of beautifully designed units containing records that are clearly labeled and impeccably organized. Toward the rear, on the left, are four listening stations where you can stack up prospective purchases and work your way through them with no pressure to hurry.

Staff member Roel de Boer has been working at the store since day one, so he knows exactly how to make people feel at ease. He has an almost infallible working knowledge of the shop's stock, plus a wider grasp of what's happening across Europe and the rest of the world. With Roel at the helm, manning the counter, you really can't go wrong and you're guaranteed to leave with a bagful of new records or, at the very least, a wealth of info. Rush Hour also run their own highly regarded label, put on parties, and manage a distribution wing, which makes them one of the most influential outfits in Amsterdam. The family that has grown up in and around the store includes talented musicians like Hunee, San Proper, Tom Trago, and many other Dutch protagonists who have gone on to make an impact globally. If you're in Amsterdam, make sure you pay Rush Hour a visit and say hello to Roel and the gang.

EUROPE

LEFT
Rush Hour's "less is more" approach to shop design is a welcome change from other cramped vinyl caverns.

12 Tónar | Reykjavik

What?	**A bit of everything, including lots of local music**
Where?	**Skólavörðustíg 15, 101 Reykjavik, Iceland**
When?	**1998**
Why?	**Step into a time warp where life moves at a slower pace**

A unique energy emanates from Iceland, traveling up from the Earth's core and drifting out through its many volcanoes. It's an island that has been responsible for some incredible musicians over the years and so you can be sure that its record shops will also be of a high caliber. 12 Tónar certainly lives up to this expectation, being one of Reykjavik's very best record outlets. Launched in 1998 by a crack team of three music enthusiasts, Lárus Jóhannesson and Johannes Ágústsson, together with Einar Sonic Kristjánsson of the legendary Icelandic rock band Singapore Sling, it has become a hub for local, national, and international visitors alike.

The music policy is eclectic, encompassing all that is great about the multifaceted art form, with a smorgasbord of local talent represented across its two floors, alongside thousands of releases from all over the world. One of 12 Tónar's key attributes is its relaxed and cozy atmosphere. From the very beginning the owners set out to create a space where people could stop by and indulge in some good-quality hanging-out time, a comfy space where customers can socialize and muse about music, life, love, and the universe. This is evident in the sofas and armchairs dotted around the store, which can be used for listening purposes or to grab a pew and chew the fat with a newfound friend or two. The shop's own special-blend espresso is also available for free to customers, which gives you even more reason to spend time there (as if the amazing music and atmosphere weren't enough). You can purchase 12 Tónar coffee beans over the counter or via their online store—surely the only record store in the world that has its own brand of coffee.

EUROPE

ABOVE
Be prepared to lose a few hours in 12 Tónar, it's that sort of place.

RIGHT
For such a small country, Iceland's music scene punches well above its weight. The country boasts a dedicated core of music lovers who celebrate the successes of local acts.

Many of Iceland's most famous musicians are known to frequent the shop—so keep an eye out for some familiar faces (Björk, Sigur Rós, múm, and many others have passed through the doors in the years since it opened)—and many Icelandic stars still spend a lot of time there. On top of all this, 12 Tónar is also a respected record label with over 70 albums making up its back catalog.

Råkk & Rålls | Oslo

What?	**An exhaustive assortment of genres**
Where?	**Stortingsgata 8, 0161 Oslo, Norway**
When?	**1993**
Why?	**For a taste of Oslo's most legendary record vendor**

Råkk & Rålls (Rock & Rolls) is a music-lover's paradise. It's the kind of place where even a noncommittal hunter will end up spending a long time searching through the racks, getting their dig on, and ending up in the depths of vinyl heaven. It all started in 1993 in Grünerløkka, an Oslo neighborhood that has become a bit of a hipster hangout in recent years. The shop was housed in a tiny space and soon outgrew its little nest, spreading its wings and venturing closer to the center of the Norwegian capital. It was in Akersgata that Råkk & Rålls achieved legendary status, thanks to its sheer size. Spread across three floors, the Akersgata spot was an absolute dream for crate-diggers, with over 150,000 records lining the walls (and staircases), from floor to ceiling in places. The cluttered store had everything from strange B-movie soundtracks to Celine Dion LPs, and it became the mecca for vinyl enthusiasts across Norway, Europe, and the rest of the world—thousands of record-collecting tourists have made the pilgrimage to the shop over the years. R&R's core ethos is simply to offer visitors a chance to discover new music, rare releases, and a ton of good stuff across a myriad genres—with virtually no filtering process besides the standard quality control asserted by all good record vendors.

In 2017 Råkk & Rålls was forced to change location due to a rent increase that squeezed them out of their three-level home. Fortunately, the owner Trond Wikborg and his staff members, André Bjørnsrud and Anette Pedersen (the manager), were able to take their business to the basement of Stortingsgata 8, where the legend continues, albeit in a slightly smaller space. Still, the exhaustive range of music on offer remains the same and the space is a little less cluttered, with better ventilation (the old spot was freezing cold in winter and sauna-esque in summer). This new location has retained some of the character of the last store and, most importantly, the attitude of the staff is still as amenable as you could wish. André and Anette are in the same band, an outfit called Ambition who specialize in hardcore. Anette is on bass, while André is the vocalist, boosting their credentials and giving customers the opportunity to meet a couple of industry veterans. Anette also played with Nasse Nøff (The Piglet) before Ambition, and she's happy to talk about her colorful past as well as help you out with any vinyl queries.

As is the case with so many record shops, once the strong reputation is established, it doesn't matter where they are based, the people will come. This is most certainly the case with Råkk & Rålls, and it will continue to be Oslo's pride and joy for a long, long time.

ABOVE
All of the stock is secondhand, with vinyl recordings being the store's best-selling stock, although they also sell DVDs, some CDs, merchandise, and lots more.

CAN Records | Copenhagen

What?	**Very best-quality, eclectic selection**
Where?	**Tullinsgade 5, 1618 Copenhagen V, Denmark**
When?	**2003**
Why?	**A record store done in a typically unique Danish way**

The Danish penchant for appreciating the simple things in life, an aspect of their culture referred to as hygge, permeates almost everything they do, and that is certainly the case in this understated, yet colorful, record shop and gallery. Martin Aalykke Kristiansen and his wife, Stine Maria Aalykke, run the show with Martin's curation of the petite space and its contents all dependent on his customers. When you take into account that many of CAN's visitors are serious vinyl fiends, then you know that the music Martin is putting out on the shelves can only be of the highest quality. This creates a supreme level of music—and makes CAN one of those very special places where the atmosphere is friendly and welcoming—combined with a mouthwatering collection of international and local releases.

The store is named after a German experimental rock band who were at the forefront of the highly influential krautrock movement back in the late 1960s. Their music was open-minded, incorporating influences from electronica to world music, with a firm psychedelic lilt and almost impossible to pigeonhole. With such an iconic group as inspiration for its name, CAN Records was on the right path from the get-go. Walk in off the

main street in Frederiksberg and you're greeted with its gallery room, the walls adorned with unusual, brightly colored prints, before you enter the second room where the records are kept. You'll probably spend hours in this space, drooling at all the immaculate recordings, as Martin holds the fort ready to answer any questions, or simply have a conversation about music or anything else you may care to discuss.

If owning and curating one of the world's best record shops wasn't enough, Martin and Stine are also accomplished artists and you can admire their work in the store's gallery. Their prints, paintings, and 3D work are unusual, intriguing, and almost certainly going to end up being carefully hung on the wall of your lounge while you listen to all the new music you picked in their store. It's a total haven and one where you will leave feeling as though your life has been made just that little bit better.

ABOVE
CAN is located in Frederiksberg. It's a cool area to spend time in, with several other record stores a short walk away.

EUROPE

DORMA 21 | Copenhagen

What?	**Various styles of electronic music**
Where?	**Salotto42, Pilestræde 52, 1112 Copenhagen, Denmark**
When?	**2012**
Why?	**It's a dream to shop there**

Beer and vinyl is always a winning combination, so you'll be pleased to know that both are readily available at this nifty little outlet in Copenhagen. As always, the Danes are well versed at doing things to a very high standard, and DORMA 21 reaps the benefits of this mentality. Owner Jacob Almanzi is an avid record collector himself and has instilled the venue with that deep-rooted passion—going to great lengths to ensure the shelves are organized so they are very easy to navigate, for example. This is a crucial aspect of record-store design that is often overlooked; at DORMA 21, it is the foundation of the shop's appeal. Built around that core of exemplary organization is the selection of music, which ranges from disco to house and techno; every single record is of the highest quality—there's no scrimping on quality there. Every record is handpicked by Jacob himself, giving the selection on offer a very personal touch.

ABOVE AND BELOW
DORMA 21 is a boutique that truly embodies the spirit of record stores, with a contemporary, Danish twist.

In March 2017, the shop moved to a new location, at a high-spec space called Salotto42 in a well-to-do district of the Danish capital. The interior design is typically Scandinavian: beautifully crafted, wooden shelf units; clean, minimal esthetics; and a calm ambience throughout. There are listening booths where you'll spend hours sifting through the mountains of quality vinyl on sale—just make sure you don't break the cardinal rule of record stores, and actually buy a few records rather than spending the whole day listening to them but not making a single purchase. Satisfied customers speak of the high level of service offered at DORMA 21, where Jacob is always at hand to give advice on new stock, as well as to provide expert knowledge on all things electronic music-wise. High praise all round for this must-visit modern store.

EUROPE

Sound Station | Copenhagen

What?	**Across the board**
Where?	**Gammel Kongevej 94, 1850 Frederiksberg, Copenhangen, Denmark**
When?	**1991**
Why?	**A grown-up record store with a warm vibe**

When you walk into Sound Station in Copenhagen it's almost like stepping into a library, such is the layout of the shop's shelves. Dark wood, floor-to-ceiling units contain most of the records stocked at the store, and they've been very carefully organized to make your browsing experience as smooth and untaxing as possible. Like its other Danish counterparts, Sound Station has a style all its own: soft lighting, a "mature" feel to the interior design, antique valve-powered record-playing equipment, and a general ambience that makes shopping there an absolute pleasure.

Sound Station occupies a street corner in the heart of Frederiksberg, one of Copenhagen's most vibrant, multicultural areas. The store has three key words dictating its identity—depth, interest, and variety, which means you can bet your bottom dollar that you'll come across something you've never heard before while trawling through the neatly arranged shelves and boxes. Rural blues? Check. Sixties' pop? Done. Weird 1980s electronica? Yep. It's all there and typically of very good quality—in fact, you can expect to pay a little bit more for the records simply because they really do go the extra mile to make sure those they sell have been loved and cared for. For anyone who gets excited at finding classic albums in mint condition, this is a total dream.

ABOVE
However obscure your tastes, chances are you will find something you're into among these wooden racks.

There are thousands of records, CDs, DVDs, and more on sale in the shop, plus they have an online hub where you can have your pick of more than 40,000 records. Having been around since 1991, Sound Station's owners have refined and perfected the art of selling records, meaning that a visit offers

RIGHT
With over 40,000 records, Sound Station is home to what is believed to be one of Denmark's biggest music collections.

you a chance to experience a top-tier vinyl emporium. Sound Station is thought to be one of the best-stocked music outlets in Denmark, and it is certainly a very important place to visit if you're keen to pick up great-quality music from a very wide range of genres.

Pet Sounds | Stockholm

What?	**Swedish indie and a variety of other great music**
Where?	**Skånegatan 53, 116 37 Stockholm, Sweden**
When?	**1979**
Why?	**Unrivaled history at one of Sweden's key record outlets**

Named after the Beach Boys' album, Pet Sounds has held its own in Stockholm for four decades and is still going strong. Life began for the infamous shop way back in 1979, when Stefan Jacobsson channeled his love for music and record collecting into a physical space that would become one of his country's most famous record stores. With prior experience working in record shops, it made sense for Stefan to get his own thing going, and, with his colleague Calle Eklund, he got Pet Sounds off the ground with the 1980s just around the corner. Calle's sister is the actress Britt Ekland, who aided the store's conception, assisting her brother to get a bank loan to fund the initial stages of the shop.

Years in the game and Stefan's unwavering passion for sharing music have kept Pet Sounds ahead of the pack in Sweden ever since it opened. The music selection is always on point, with Swedish indie a specialty, as well as the full spectrum of popular music, dance releases, and a whole host of worldwide sounds— if eclectic is what you want, then look no farther. Staff are always at hand for advice and tips, or a simple chat about anything and everything. Stefan has a reputation for being slightly frosty at first, as some record-store owners can be; however, once you've penetrated that cool exterior, you're in the Pet Sounds' club for life, so try not to take it personally and persevere if you feel rejected at first, he really is a big softie.

ABOVE
Pet Sounds is one of Sweden's most influential record stores.

As you may expect, a place that has been around since 1979 has seen a fair amount of famous faces in its time. Besides its Hollywood connection with Britt Ekland being there at its birth, Pet Sounds has also been visited by musical luminaries like John Peel, Bryan Ferry, Björk, and Elvis Costello—plus bands such as Coldplay, Blur, and Oasis have performed there. Stefan has direct contact with many of Sweden's best-known artists, which means that the lineups for special events are always top-notch and the concerts organized by Pet Sounds often sell out whether they announce the performers or not—a sure sign of the store's popularity and how much trust music fans have in its ability to curate excellent events.

At one stage Pet Sounds had branches across the nation in Gothenburg, Norrköping, and Halmstad. Now focused solely on Stockholm, you can find the main outlet in Soder, one of the city's most stylish and happening islands, with its sister bar and restaurant located diagonally opposite the record store—the ideal place to enjoy a post-digging cocktail. It goes without saying that Pet Sounds is a crucial destination for any music-lover or vinyl fiend.

Snickars Records | Stockholm

What?	Eclectic: African and Latin to upfront dance music
Where?	Hökens gata 11, 116 46 Stockholm, Sweden
When?	1995
Why?	A shop designed for leisurely record shopping

1995, a vintage year for many forms of contemporary music and the year when Snickars Records came into being. Owner Mika Snickars had already been collecting and playing vinyl for quite some time before he decided to set up his very own store. Putting his heart and soul into getting it off the ground, Mika's hard work paid off and was the catalyst behind many years of success. What makes Snickars Records such a great space is the laid-back atmosphere; people are encouraged to lounge on the sofas and chairs dotted around the shop floor and perusing the racks of records can be done at leisure. Rushing almost feels criminal here, when there are so many opportunities to stop and chat to other eager vinyl enthusiasts, or you can simply chill alone and enjoy the atmosphere. You can't help but slow down your pace and enjoy the present moment, especially when there's such a glorious selection of music on offer: upfront dance music is placed side by side with African disco, jazz, hip hop, and numerous other genres, all of which are chosen by Mika himself. Sharing a space with the Konstart gallery (owned by Mika's girlfriend), you enter Snickars Records through the art displays and encounter the smart, minimal, and slightly quirky store. The Scandinavian approach to interior design is in full effect at Snickars, with beautiful wooden display shelves and sleek racks lining the shop floor. It's a haven, a social hub, and a space where you can really lose yourself.

Mika's credentials as a DJ include winning the Swedish leg of the DMC Championships back in 1998, and touring with his crew The Scratchaholics for over 15 years. You'll find him behind the counter at Snickars, ready and willing to dole out advice and information to anyone who needs it. A Swedish publication once called him a man of few words, but it would be more appropriate to say that Mika prefers to let the music do the talking. And why not when there are so many life-affirming melodies and infectious rhythms out there in the musical universe?

Hard Wax | Berlin

What?	**Underground electronic music**
Where?	**Paul-Lincke-Ufer 44A, 10999 Berlin, Germany**
When?	**1989**
Why?	**To witness the record shop in its optimum form**

Anything connected to the great Mark Ernestus is almost guaranteed to have a seal of quality. In case you haven't heard of him, Mark founded legendary techno outfit and label Basic Channel with fellow German Moritz Von Oswald, pioneering the early dub techno sound back in the early nineties. He opened Hard Wax all the way back in 1989 following on from his art school project Kumplenest 3000, a pub which he opened in 1987. Three decades since it was opened, Hard Wax remains one of the most respected electronic music shops in Berlin, with its reputation spreading worldwide.

The music selection on offer centers mainly around techno, underground electronica, and experimental sounds from around the globe. With its sparse, bleak interior the Berlin store is perfectly suited to the music it stocks—bare concrete and untreated wooden fixtures which are now par for the course, are intrinsic to the make up of this shop. Visitors can sit themselves down at one of the listening spots, settling down on a comfy stool while they work through their fresh pile of potential new purchases.

The atmosphere is welcoming, but perhaps a tad intimidating to the uninitiated. Buyers at Hard Wax are very picky when it comes to the music they put on sale, which has earned them a tough reputation among distributors. This is a shop for the heads, where famous techno DJs such as Marcel Dettmann have worked behind the counter and where anyone who wants the very best, high-quality techno will pay a visit. In fact, if techno is your bag, then it really doesn't get any better than this.

EUROPE

RIGHT
In a city that is home to some of the best DJs in the world, it's fitting that it has one of the world's best record shops to serve them.

OYE Records | Berlin

What?	**House, techno, disco, and all that good stuff**
Where?	**Friedelstrasße 49, 12047 Berlin, Germany**
When?	**2002**
Why?	**Superb music and top recommendations, as only Berlin can offer**

O ne look at its bright exterior in Neukölln tells you OYE Records is where you want to be digging for new music, for several hours at the very least. Originally starting out as a small outlet in the lower ground floor of a house in Prenzlauer Berg, OYE was founded in 2002 by Lovis Willenberg, who launched the store with a focus on Latin and Brazilian sounds. As time went by, staff members Markus Lindner (aka Delfonic) and Tinko Rohst became part-owners, and OYE began evolving into its current incarnation, with a second location joining that first outlet in the late 2000s. The focus changed to meet demand and it is now a formidable proprietor of electronic music, mostly house and techno, with a good selection of disco and other such treats on offer.

ABOVE
Look out for regular in-store gigs at OYE.

Markus is typically clinical, though equally passionate, in his curation of the store's wares—you will not find a single dud release; everything is of the finest quality with a carefully curated selection of labels and artists who have universal respect from record buyers and fanatical diggers alike. All the staff members are happy to offer their expertise, with many customers commenting on their recommendation skills. What really makes OYE a special place is its connection to the local scene; it has a reciprocal relationship with many Berlin-based musicians, inspiring the launch of several labels and maintaining a close, productive relationship with all of them. The list includes the mighty Disco Halal and Moscoman, Max Graef and Box Aus Holz, and Delfonic's own Money $ex Records, plus the shop's own OYE Edits—a home for cheeky reworks produced by the store's extended family.

With several listening posts and a relaxed, friendly vibe, OYE Records is visited by wave after wave of tourists, especially during the summer months when Berlin really comes to life. It is also a popular haunt in winter, though, thanks to its impeccable selections, together with regular in-store gigs. In fact, the store has hosted over 200 shows since it first opened, mainly because the owners grew tired of promoting events externally and saw the shop as the perfect remedy to their woes. With an excellent sound system, intimate surroundings, and a switched-on, up-for-it crowd at every gig, OYE's in-stores are always hugely popular and help set it apart from many of its rivals.

Spacehall | Berlin

What?	**Heavy metal through to heavyweight techno**
Where?	**Zossener Straße 35, Kreuzberg, 10961 Berlin, Germany**
When?	**1991**
Why?	**Big, dark, and oh so "Berlin"—it's a totally immersive experience like no other**

One of Berlin's biggest record stores, Spacehall has achieved cult status in its Kreuzberg home, with over 20 years in the game. Peter, the owner, originally set up the shop with his wife in 1991 at Zossener Straße 34. In the years that have passed since that first venture, which was comprised around 1,500-plus CDs and vinyl being sold from a basement, the Spacehall empire has taken over the retail spaces either side of 34, with the record store now at 35 and the CD outlet at 33, while the original location is now a café.

Inside the main record shop, you'll be greeted by merchandise and flyers before hitting the meditative corridor, which leads to the house and techno section. It's all very "Berlin"—low lighting, exposed brick pillars, and very black indeed. While perusing the shelves and racks, you'll become immersed in the experience, forgetting the outside world within minutes and getting lost in a new dimension, full of magical, hypnotic black wax. This absorbing, darkened interior is all part of the plan, as the owners want to encourage customers to lose themselves in the record-digging experience—such a space also inhibits communication, which means the atmosphere is perhaps less sociable than a lot of other record stores. Still, this counts as a positive, reinforcing Spacehall's ability to submerge you in its impeccable selection. Shopping for vinyl really becomes an *experience*, and one which you will not forget in a hurry.

Though it may sometimes feel a little intimidating, Spacehall almost always seems to have a buzz in the air. The shop is often over-run with eager music-hunters, and the staff are always on the move, restocking the shelves with fresh new releases from the stockroom all the time. The music policy is open and democratic, so as not to alienate anybody—the crowd is always very diverse, from older gentleman looking to bolster their collection of rare rockabilly vinyl to the fairweather vinyl collector who wants to grab the latest trendy techno release. Everyone is welcome at Spacehall, and that is what makes it such a special place.

EUROPE

Public Possession | Munich

What?	**The finest underground electronic cuts**
Where?	**Klenzestraße 16, 80469 Munich, Germany**
When?	**2013**
Why?	**A cultural hub that's changing the face of Munich's electronic music scene**

Marvin Schuhmann and Valentino Betz are like a two-man creative army who seem to have little regard for pigeonholes, and rightly so—defining one's self with a predetermined title can be very limiting. On the contrary, the two men have liberated themselves with a confident approach to life that encompasses many different disciplines and endeavors, culminating in a mini-empire of sorts. This is Public Possession, and Marvin and Valentino are DJs, label bosses, bookers, art directors, publishers, and sometime caterers (when their shop is hosting in-store gigs). It all

ABOVE
For information about great music, dial these digits.

appears to come so naturally to the duo; their energy is fueled by their incessant passion for music and creativity—and it's paid off as Public Possession is widely regarded as one of the best record stores in Munich. With no prior experience of running a shop before, their project could have been a total disaster, but when there's genuine love at the heart of your business, success is bound to come your way.

Since its launch in 2013, the store has gone from strength to strength, despite Munich's music scene being nowhere near as strong as that of some of its German counterparts: Berlin, Hamburg, and Frankfurt, for example. Representing the duo's distinct tastes, Public Possession is widely considered to be one of Munich's true gems, punching way above its weight in terms of size. The modest space has been neatly designed and laid out, with an unfussy arrangement of shelves featuring tons of the latest quirky, underground vinyl releases—records you just can't

find elsewhere in the German city—plus a few well-placed palm trees, which give it a fresh, homely (and slightly tropical) feel. The cozy space has been used for live gigs ever since the shop opened, and the list of performers who've graced the decks there reads like a festival lineup—a very cool festival where 99 percent of the crowd is discerning, yet up for a good old party. Guests have included Young Marco, Optimo Espacio, Keinemusik's Adam Port, Tornado Wallace, the Zenker Brothers, Suzanne Kraft, and many more international and local selectors.

Something that Marvin and Valentino do very well is express their offbeat sense of humor through the graphic design of their flyers and promotional materials, as well as in their mixes and music (the two men make up two-thirds of production outfit Tambien). This gives the spot its strong identity and helps to unify the many divisions of their beloved empire. So, with love, passion, creativity, and humor driving it forward, Public Possession continues to grow and provide a base for Munich's small, yet potent, electronic music scene. Inspiring and enlightening, it's a magnificent example of what's possible when you put your heart and soul into a record store.

Side One | Warsaw

What?	**Polish electronica to deep dubby techno**
Where?	**Chmielna 21, 00-001 Warsaw, Poland**
When?	**2005**
Why?	**The information center for Warsaw's music scene and a cultural hub**

Run by Wojtek Żdanuk (aka DJ WWW), Side One is the jewel in Warsaw's record-store crown. Small in size, but big in character and influence, it has been open since 2005 and acts not only as the epicenter of the city's record-buying community, but also as the HQ for a whole host of music industry heads: promoters, label owners, producers, and many more. On any given day of the week you can walk into the shop, located in a small courtyard in the center of Warsaw, and encounter various Polish music bods musing over the ins and outs of their scene, or simply catching up with each other's goings-on. It's a social hub where connections are made and reinforced, galvanizing the city's ever-fertile industry. Though small, Side One never feels cluttered, thanks to the nifty layout—records are carefully positioned in boxes, shelves, and racks so as to avoid disorder. There are a couple of deck chairs set out so you can really relax if you wish; this is a shop where there is no need to rush around frantically rummaging through the selection on offer. It's more of a chill-out spot where you can spend the whole day listening to music and chatting at your leisure.

BELOW
Side One gives a great snapshot of Warsaw's culture scene.

EUROPE

Side One's support for the local scene has transcended its four walls to now include a record label called S1, the first release (by Eltron John) landing in 2013. More

ABOVE
Look out for records from the store's own label, S1.

recently, the label dropped a 12-track compilation to celebrate their 10th anniversary. This milestone was also marked by a party thrown by Boiler Room. Now considered to be a Polish institution, Side One is without a doubt the country's premier record store.

LEFT
On the walls, you'll see old records that have been repurposed as clocks and, in keeping with the horological theme, Happyfeet also sells old Czech Plim watches that have been refurbished.

Happyfeet | Prague

What?	**An eclectic selection of new and secondhand vinyl**
Where?	**Vodičkova 704/36, 110 00 Nové Město, Prague, Czech Republic**
When?	**2007**
Why?	**Supraphon, Opus, AND Panton recordings… what more do you need?**

If you don't know much about the Czech music scene, then this is definitely the place for you. The owner Magdalena Zemanová has created a delightful space which is located in a very easy-to-reach part of the city, surrounded by posh food stores, trendy bars and cafés, and even a Persian rug emporium. Its downtown location, in Lucerna Palace right next to Wenceslas Square, makes it a popular choice for locals and tourists alike. The first Happyfeet premises opened in 2007; it then moved to Opatovická in 2008 and on to the Roxy club in 2010. The shop has been in the passage of Lucerna Palace (Vaclav Havel's family building) since 2011. It's important to note that Happyfeet is pretty small, so space is at a premium when it gets busy, but this only adds to the atmosphere and creates a sociable environment in which to excavate rare finds.

Magdalena is a treasure herself, being not only an expert when it comes to Czech and Slovak music, but also a tremendously talented DJ and a genuinely beautiful soul to boot—if you're fluent in Czech, then check out her TED Talk on YouTube. When you're in her store, you'll feel at ease and able to ask her anything, no matter how trivial it may seem. Such is the welcoming atmosphere that kids as young as eight (her youngest customer) pop in to spend their pocket money on records. Magdalena is patient, full of information, and approachable—just what you want from a record-shop owner.

One of Happyfeet's key strengths is its selection of old Supraphon, Opus, and Panton pressings. These three labels were the main state-owned outlets for Czechoslovak recordings, and Happyfeet has a great collection of their releases, from the weird to the wonderful, classical to contemporary, and everything in between. Alongside the local delicacies you'll find international rock from the 1960s up to the present day and a small, yet impressive, jazz, soul, and funk selection. This sweet little Czech store is the perfect combination of quirky and welcoming, and seriously good value for rarities, oddities, and classics.

ABOVE
Small but perfectly formed, Happyfeet has an excellently eclectic approach to the records it stocks.

DiG | Moscow

What?	**DnB to classical and a variety of Russian delights**
Where?	**Staraya Basmannaya, 15Ac15, Moscow, Russia**
When?	**2010**
Why?	**A unique community-focused space in the Russian capital**

Petr Chinavat and Ivan Smekalin* have created a sanctuary in Moscow, their hometown. It's a space where audiophiles rub shoulders with people who are simply intrigued by the store, with its bright green front comprised of repurposed wooden pallets. DiG opened in 2010 and, in the time since then, it has become a hub for all kinds of music-related activity. What Petr and Ivan want most from their shop is to form genuine friendships with their customers, while also introducing them to new music. It's a simple, yet very powerful, ethos in a city where it can be difficult to operate outside of superficial societal norms.

Visitors can expect a wide range of vinyl delights, which reflect Petr and Ivan's eclectic tastes, ranging from Goldie to Mariah Carey, Aphex Twin to Snoop Dogg through to Can, classical, jazz, and a myriad Russian disco cuts, plus many more local releases. The mark of a truly special record store is its ability to galvanize the local scene and to inspire artists and collectors. DiG does this exceptionally well and has become the nerve center for Moscow's ever-growing underground scene. In particular, they push local musicians through their regular events series, as well as buying in a plethora of releases from Russian labels.

ABOVE
DiG prides itself on supporting the local scene.

The space itself is modern and well lit, with 3,000-plus records neatly arranged on wooden shelves. Though it's not huge, there is plenty of space to accommodate those moments when the shop receives a rush of customers, as you may experience during one of their many in-store gigs, for example. The staff are super-friendly, with a good grasp of English, and always at hand to assist visitors, whether they're ultra-nerdy collectors or people who know very little about music—everyone is welcomed and given the same attentive, caring response. Their knowledge extends beyond musical recordings and into technology, which can sometimes be hard to get hold of locally.

Petr and Ivan have cultivated a community around DiG, an engaged group of creative activists who have a progressive view of the world and have found a home among like-minded people at the store. This community participates in their events, from in-store performances to their innovative Sunday Vinyl School, where punters listen to records in the dark and then spend some time discussing what they've just heard. Books are also an important part of DiG's appeal; with a selection of publications from independent distributors on sale, these include rarities, comics, photo-books, and a wide variety of other such tomes covering music, counterculture, biographies, art, and lots more. DiG is an extraordinary place which has established a strong identity and a dedicated following, bringing a distinct and consistently inspiring ethos to the Russian capital.

*Gregory Eniosov was also intrinsic to the conception of DiG; he passed away on August 16, 2016. RIP.

Analog Kültür | Istanbul

What?	Turkish recordings, secondhand international releases, and vintage equipment
Where?	Şahkulu Mah. Serdar-ı Ekrem Cad. Seraskerci Şıkmazı 4/A Beyoğlu, Istanbul, Turkey
When?	2014
Why?	An expertly curated selection of Turkish delights

If you want to know all the latest ins and outs of Istanbul's vibrant music scene, then you must pay Analog Kültür a visit. That's if you can find it... Like a few of the world's most respected record stores, it's a bit tricky to find, thanks to its clandestine basement location somewhere in Beyoğlu, the hip part of town (of course), on one of its coolest streets. Perseverance is key here and lots of it, but the slabs of shiny black gold you'll find at the end of your exhaustive hunt will be more than worth it. Analog Kültür's owner Kaan Düzürat has made sure that your reward for tracking down his shop is a superlative selection of releases from local artists, coupled with a delectable collection of secondhand international music that ranges from afro funk through to prog rock.

The shop is intimate and the kind of place where you'll easily make friends with other customers, if you don't end up having a deep and meaningful with Kaan himself, who is always at hand to fill you in on the store's varied stock. A great accompaniment to the records on offer is the vintage equipment that is also sold on site, from old tape decks to turntables and synths. The shop also contains a recording studio where local musicians drop in and get busy collaborating on exciting new projects or helming their own solo productions. A buzz often fills the store due to the creative energy that spills out of the recording space. All in all, it's a cultural hub and a local institution that has no doubt bolstered Istanbul's music scene. A place that is well worth visiting if you're in Turkey.

BELOW
Even the most jaded crate digger will find something new and exciting at Analog Kültür.

RIGHT Afro-Synth Records, Johannesburg

Chapter Three

The Middle East and Africa

Middle East

The Flip Side | Dubai

What?	**Local acts, plus a host of international releases**
Where?	**Unit 71, Alserkal Avenue, Dubai, United Arab Emirates**
When?	**2017**
Why?	**A fresh young store with huge potential and a determined outlook**

As the only independent record shop in Dubai, The Flip Side is playing a key role in developing the country's music scene, acting as a hub for artists and collectors to congregate and share their love for music. Owned by Shadi Megallaa, the store opened on May 21, 2017, and quickly became the HQ for much of Dubai's electronic music activity. Shadi was born in Egypt and raised in the United Arab Emirates, where he got into skating and BMX'ing—music is intrinsically linked to both these street sports and it wasn't long before he was making tapes with all the music he loved. At the age of 14, Shadi got into DnB, and so began a lifelong love affair with electronic music. A move to Brooklyn in his twenties cemented his love for music in all its forms and his career as a DJ began to flourish. When he returned to Abu Dhabi he set up Ark to Ashes, a record label that represents his love of deep house and dub reggae, inspired by the great Lee "Scratch" Perry. Starting up his record store, The Flip Side, was actually first suggested by Shadi's parents, who could see he was unhappy working at his father's architecture firm.

Supporting local artists is paramount and a core ethos of the shop, so, when you peruse the crates, you will come across a large percentage of releases from acts and labels based in Dubai and the UAE. Shadi's own Ark to Ashes label, plus outlets like Volt Music, Bedouin Records, and Boogie Box are showcased alongside a wide range of international records: jazz, soul, hip hop, ambient, and an extensive selection of electronic music. The Flip Side is spacious and modern inside, with four listening stations and all the records neatly organized in racks dotted around the shop floor. It has a homely feel; once inside, you'll want to spend a decent amount of time digging, chilling, and discovering. Dubai-based graffiti artist Sya One has adorned the walls and dividers with his handiwork, adding to the store's cultural value. Shadi is involved in lots of different musical ventures—for example, there's a plethora of in-store gigs featuring international guests and he has his own radio show, "The Shady Shadow Show." There is also Dub Ethics, hosted by Sami Ism and Shadi M, which celebrates dub music in all its forms, plus Astral Travelling, hosted by Hani J and Shadi, which ventures into all things cosmic, from boogie, funk, and disco to house music and so on. The Flip Side record label is in its early stages, and there are more plans to develop the shop and build its connections with the local scene. An exciting, dynamic young store with fire in its belly and a clear focus on the future.

LEFT
The Flip Side logo. The shop is
spearheading the resurgence
of vinyl in the UAE.

BELOW
With support for local artists and labels, an associated radio show, and
plenty of in-store gigs, The Flip Side goes above and beyond the call of
duty in its mission to nuture Dubai's underground music scene.

Chico Records | Beirut

What?	**Arabic music from the 1960s and 1970s**
Where?	**Sadat-Sidani intersection, Beirut 0113 7432, Lebanon**
When?	**1964**
Why?	**For a discerning dip into Arabic music and culture**

Chico Records was established by Khatchik Mardirian in October 1964. Back then it was called Pick of the Pops, but in 1976 a bomb destroyed the shop sign, and Khatchik (who is nicknamed Chico) never replaced it with a new one. So, the store simply became known as Chico's. It is currently owned by Diran Mardirian, Khatchik's youngest son, who has been working there since he was just 12 years old. Developing a deep love for music through his experiences at the store, it was inevitable that Diran would take over the reins when his father decided to hand it down to his offspring.

Beirut has a strong music scene, operating across genres that range from blues and soul through to electronic, and its international outlook means it is ever evolving and always has its finger on the pulse. Chico Records focuses on 1960s and 1970s jazz, soul, and rock, with an extensive Arabic music selection that is second to none. Diran and his father have been industrious and unwavering in their curation of local music, making it one of the primary sources for Arabic releases in the region, if not the entire world. They have contributed over 1,500 Arabic releases to Discogs and continue to supply the online portal with new, rare, and difficult-to-get-hold of pressings whenever they can. Diran's knowledge is invaluable; there aren't many

ABOVE
Chico Records is an authority on Arabic music.

people who can lay claim to having such an in-depth experience of music curation in Beirut, especially from such an early age. He is assisted by Ramzi Abou Ammo who manages the 15,000-strong DVD library—the collection focuses on world and cult movies, as well as the classics and contemporary cinema.

Inside the two-storey shop there are rows of wooden racks and metal shelf units carrying 7-inches and 12-inches, plus lots of CDs and a few cassettes. Listening stations look out onto the street, so you'll be entertained visually as well as aurally when you start sifting through your prospective purchases. There's coffee and tea on tap, together with the offer of good conversation with Diran himself, a man who is well versed in how to keep record buyers happy—on colder days, he cracks open the whiskey! Chico's is a sweet little spot that merges Beirut's past with its present in a wonderfully inspiring way.

Africa

Mazeeka Samir Fouad | Cairo

What?	**Old Egyptian releases, classical, plus vintage audio equipment, and much more**
Where?	**Ismail Mohamed Street, Zamalek (second floor, above Metro grocery store), Cairo, Egypt**
When?	**2012**
Why?	**A ramshackle space that is completely unique and unusual**

Tucked away in a rough and ready shopping mall, Mazeeka Samir Fouad is a remnant of record shops of the past. It's a chaotic, disorganized storage space for music, vintage music equipment, Polaroids, black and white postcards, pictures, paperback pulp fiction, and a myriad other collectables, mostly from the past. The walls and storefront are adorned with classic posters featuring Egypt's finest, and you can buy any number of old gramophones and ouds (guitar-esque local instruments), should you wish. In fact, it is said that Mazeeka has Cairo's biggest collection of antique record players. On the busy shelves there are dusty old hi-fis, TVs, and turntables, as well as the more esthetically pleasing gramophones with their ornate horns. The music selection is so different from anything you'll find anywhere else in the world that it's more than worth a visit. There are old shellac 78s (mistakenly called "rock records") and a wide range of 45s, 7-inches, and 12-inches in varying condition—in fact, some are so crackly that John Doran, editor of *The Quietus*, thought they might have sand in the grooves. Classical music, 1920s and 1930s Arabic releases, infamous Egyptian band Les Petits Chats, and a variety of other unusual treats are stocked at Mazeeka—just be patient, as you'll have do a fair amount of sifting through badly organized, disheveled piles.

According to Mazeeka's manager, Ahmed Hamada, most of the records have been gathered up from abandoned houses around Cairo and old record shops over generations. Interestingly, many were rescued from the library of the Khedivial Royal Opera House while it was burning down in a terrible fire in 1971. Mazeeka is a fascinating space with a life of its own that demands you spend time really digging deep into its collection. If you can afford to ship one home, purchasing a gramophone or oud is highly recommended…

THE MIDDLE EAST AND AFRICA

Jazzhole | Lagos

What?	**Jazz, vintage equipment, books, and cake!**
Where?	**168 Awolowo Road, Ikoyi, Lagos, Nigeria**
When?	**1980s**
Why?	**It's truly one of a kind...**

Jazzhole is a legendary Lagos spot that combines selling records and books with a café. Its reputation stretches way beyond Nigeria and Africa to court vinyl enthusiasts from all over the planet. The legend lies in the esthetics, the atmosphere, and the extraordinary music and books on offer, some of which you won't be able to find anywhere else in the world. Jazzhole is intrinsic to the creative community in Nigeria and has close links with musicians, artists, authors, and many other members of the vibrant local scene. With this as its foundation, alongside the deeply ingrained passion of the store's owners, Jazzhole has become a seminal space. It feels like a library, albeit one in which you can really relax and ease into the shopping experience—there's no hushed, awkward atmosphere, just good vibes and warmth.

Kunle Tejuoso set up Jazzhole as an offshoot of Glendora Books, also based in Lagos. Initially, the aim was to supply the growing number of international residents who were migrating to his hometown. However, as an avid music-lover himself, he began to dig deeper into indigenous music. Mr Tejuoso is now considered to be an historian of African music, heritage, and culture, striving to preserve the legacy of his nation's incredibly diverse musical history and passing on his knowledge to the younger generation. Jazzhole is at the epicenter of his efforts, providing a space where young artists can come and listen to music, read books on its history, and speak to the man himself, who is always at hand to pass down all his priceless knowledge.

The shop is also used for live gigs, with an endless list of local acts appearing, so keeping the lineage strong. Mr Tejuoso's store is a great source of inspiration for Lagos' creatives, and has played a key role is keeping the city's music scene alive and kicking. Records are casually piled up on the floor, such is the free-spirited nature of this outlet. Grab a delicious juice or a coffee with a slice of cake, kick back, and get into your groove. So relaxed is the atmosphere that customers are invited to play DJ if they wish, with the turntables in the shop open to anyone who cares to throw a record on and pump it up (or turn it down), to influence the mood of the store while shopping. As an experience Jazzhole is unlike any other record store in the world, and as a cultural phenomenon, it is one of the most important enterprises in Africa.

THIS PAGE
Don't leave here without familiarizing yourself with one of the best selections of jùjú and highlife music you will find.

Jimmy's Record Store | Nairobi

What?	**Excellent Kenyan music and lots more besides**
Where?	**Stall No. 570, Kenyatta Market, Ngummo Nairobi, Kenya**
When?	**1989**
Why?	**Grilled meat, local music, and Jimmy himself**

James "Jimmy" Rugami has been selling records since 1989, and his store has earned itself a global rep since it first opened. Based at Stall 570 at Kenyatta Market, in Nairobi, it is a small yet commanding outlet, with the charismatic Jimmy keeping customers engaged and informed throughout the day. He was once a teacher, then moved into the clothing business before finally settling on vinyl retail in the late 1980s—and that is where his heart truly lies. The location of the shop alone sets it apart from many of its counterparts around the world, as it's tucked away down an alleyway in the market, opposite a butcher's (which sells mouth-watering grilled meats). In fact, the smell of grilled meat, known locally as *nyama choma*, fills the air. There's a buzz surrounding the stall—the kind of transient energy that you can only experience in a market. In many respects, the shop holds true to the roots of record selling: small, independent, unassuming, and built on a devotion to collecting and sharing vinyl.

Jimmy's has achieved widespread notoriety in recent years, with the resurgence in record collecting having a direct effect on the stall, as well as attention from international artists like Auntie Flo. Having support from established musicians has placed Jimmy's on the international stage and encouraged visitors from far and wide to drop in. On April 22, 2017, Jimmy's became the first spot in East Africa to celebrate Record Store Day, which prompted the addition of a bigger space a few doors down from the original stall to accommodate more buyers and more stock.

At Stall 570, you'll find East African 7-inches and 12-inches, organized in a caring manner—for instance, the Kenyan section is arranged according to local languages: Luo, Kamba, Luhya, and Swahili. It is a tight space, but not a claustrophobic one. Jimmy says he owns over 50,000 records from a comprehensive variety of genres and nationalities; he now has three spaces within Kenyatta Market and is training his son, Ndegwa, to take over the business when he retires. Ndegwa has a lot to live up to; Jimmy's is Kenya's pride and joy.

BELOW
Jimmy's is a treasure trove of gems for lovers of African music and he supplies vinyl obsessives from around the world.

Afro-Synth Records | Johannesburg

What?	**South African music, bubblegum, kwaito, plus lots more**
Where?	**25 Albrecht Street, Maboneng/Jeppe, 2094 Johannesburg, South Africa**
When?	**2016**
Why?	**For an unpretentious glimpse into the world of African music**

African music has been steadily picking up more and more support in recent years, and rightly so. There is such a rich and diverse scene across the entire continent, and it's almost always overlooked in the West, especially at the commercial end of the spectrum. However, the tide has been changing, and if you're keen to learn more about Africa's highly fertile and influential music scene, then Afro-Synth is the place for you. Run by DJ Okapi, who began blogging about his own collection before starting an online store in 2015, Afro-Synth specializes in South African and African releases—especially those from the 1980s. DJ Okapi's deep love for the music produced by his fellow Africans floods every aspect of his beloved shop, and he is always there behind the counter ready to impart his knowledge to anyone who asks him a question.

ABOVE
The interesting color scheme is inspired by the shop's logo.

If you've never heard of bubblegum or kwaito, then get yourself down to Afro-Synth and indulge in a few hours of listening, digging, and chatting with Okapi. Inside the cozy, intimate venue, you'll find neatly arranged shelves and racks, with black walls and yellow trimming that reflect the colors in Afro-Synth's logo. The vibe is unpretentious and inclusive; in fact, it couldn't be any less intimidating, especially with someone as friendly and sociable as Okapi at the helm. Afro-Synth is located right next to the Museum of African Design, so you can spend a day visiting both spots, filling your mind with Africa's aural and visual delights. Get down there on a Sunday to catch one of the shop's lively in-store gigs. Okapi is closely affiliated with Rush Hour Records (see page 51), in Amsterdam, and worked on a compilation of African electronica with Rush Hour's boss man, Antal Heitlager, called *Pantsula! The Rise Of Electronic Dance Music In South Africa, 1988–90*. His international reach also includes a close connection with YouTube broadcasters, Boiler Room, and gigs as far afield as China, Leeds, and Lyon. Afro-Synth also has its own record-label branch, giving rare African pressings a new lease of life and pushing the local scene.

Okapi's unwavering love for his nation's music has given birth to a place that is not only breathing life into South Africa's scene, but also building a community around the globe, with fervent support from beyond his country's borders. A sure-fire example of how music can transcend imaginary borders to unify humanity— it's a special little place, indeed.

THE MIDDLE EAST AND AFRICA

Mabu Vinyl | Cape Town

What?	**Rock to dance to classical and beyond**
Where?	**2 Rheede Street, Gardens, Cape Town, 8001, South Africa**
When?	**2001**
Why?	**The *Searching For Sugar Man* connection alone is enough to warrant a visit**

Mabu Vinyl grew out of Cape Town's popular Kloof Street bric-a-brac store, Kloofmart, which was run by Johan Vosloo. His son, Jacques, opened the record section at the back of Kloofmart in 2001, but it wasn't long before this moved to its own plot just a few stores away. In October 2003, Mabu Vinyl moved farther down the road to premises in the Buitenkloof Centre on the corner of Kloof Street and Buitensingel Street. A month later Stephen Segerman joined Jacques in the shop, adding CDs, DVDs, and cassettes to the already huge selection of records that fills every corner of this fantastically decorated store.

In January 2008, Mabu Vinyl upped sticks once more, ending up at 2 Rheede Street, in Gardens, where it is still going strong. Jacques and Stephen run things behind the scenes (and in-store too) with Day Manager, Brian Currin, who has been with Mabu Vinyl since 2014. Mabu also employs an Evening Manager, Mayibuye Ntsatha (aka Mighty). Other friendly faces you can expect to meet at the counter include Landi Degenaar and Chris Orner. Tons of different genres are available for purchase, including a plethora of independent releases from South African artists (mostly on CD), plus everything you could wish to see, from heavy metal to classical, comedy, blues, soundtracks, and lots, lots more. A bonus is that the price range is pretty broad, so, even if you don't have much cash in your pocket, you will more than likely be able to pick something up, which is quite rare in the world of record stores these days.

The decor is bright and colorful, with LP covers and photographs adorning all the walls. This creates a bold collage of imagery and gives the shop its distinctive character—even the hand-drawn signage that divides the different genres is colorful. One of Mabu's main claims to fame is that it was featured in the Oscar-winning music documentary *Searching For Sugar Man*, the story of the re-emergence of Sixto Rodriguez. Co-owner Stephen Segerman was one of the two South Africans who were trying to track down the mysterious American folk singer whose album *Cold Fact* was a staple in South African record collections, but who was believed dead following an apparent suicide many years

ABOVE
Legendary DJ
Gilles Peterson
paying a visit to
Mabu Vinyl.

LEFT
Brian Currin mans
the counter.

before. When the film was made, Stephen was a co-owner of Mabu Vinyl, so the Cape
Town sections of the film were largely shot inside and around the store. As a result of the
worldwide popularity of Sixto Rodriguez following the film, Mabu Vinyl now welcomes
visitors from all over the world who come to visit, grab a selfie at the entrance, and buy
any Rodriguez memorabilia that's sold inside. Mabu Vinyl is a favorite of many Cape
Town dwellers and international collectors. The shop has a happy family behind it, who
keep the atmosphere jubilant; the music on sale is top-quality and it maintains a great
optimistic outlook that makes it a lovely place to shop and hang out.

3

ABOVE Paradise
Records, Chengdu

Chapter Four

Asia and Australasia

ABOVE ZudRangMa Records, Bangkok

Asia

New Gramophone House | New Delhi

What?	**A wide range of Indian music, soundtracks, and other recordings, plus refurbished gramophones and audio equipment**
Where?	**31-B, Pleasure Garden Market, Opposite Moti Cinema, Main Road, Chandni Chowk, Delhi-110006, India**
When?	**1930**
Why?	**The only store of its kind in the world**

This quaint little shop in India's bustling capital is a haven for old audio equipment. One of the oldest stores featured in the book, it was founded in 1930 by the late Bhagwan Dass Rajpal, who opened the first New Gramophone House in the Anarkali Bazaar, in Lahore. In 1947, the year of India's Partition, the store moved to Delhi where it has remained, going through a rollercoaster journey to get to where it is today. For almost 50 years, NGH was at the epicenter of India's vinyl industry, supplying records to HMV and importing gramophone needles and spare parts, with a strong client base and connections throughout the entire country. Bollywood soundtracks were hugely popular, and the majority of their range of 78s, 45s, and 12-inches came from Indian artists. However, in the 1980s, things began to slow down and, by the mid-1990s, the vinyl market was on its knees—so much so that the manufacture of records ceased in India. Delhi went from having over 100 record stores to virtually none, apart from NGH, as well as Shah Music, Maharaja Lal & Sons, Bercos, and a few more. NGH itself downsized, operating out of just one floor in the building where it once had the ground, first, and second floors. Today, the climate has changed, as global record sales are on the rise again, although most Bollywood soundtracks that have been pressed to vinyl are produced overseas.

New Gramophone House is now owned and managed by Bhagwan Dass' son Ramesh Rajpal and Anuj Rajpal, his grandson. Like many of the world's more unusual shops, it is quite hard to find. An HMV-esque banner hints at the location—inside you go, up some stairs, past a shoe store, then up another staircase where you finally enter the record shop, which is quite a sight. The shelves are lined with records, but there are also lots of beautifully refurbished gramophones with shiny, gold-colored horns glistening under the cold strip lighting. You'll find around 20,000 records in store, and Anuj speaks proudly of the thousands more kept in his storehouse. The ambience is a juxtaposition of warm, crackly 78s piped through the vintage players and the frenetic sounds of the surrounding businesses. Alongside the film scores and Indian pop releases, you'll find a dizzying array of unusual recordings, including snake-charmer music and religious readings in a variety of local dialects, as well as books, turntables, and audio equipment. The shop also repairs old gramophones and turntables. NGH is one of the world's leading collectors of Indian music in its physical form, with traditional and contemporary styles being archived and given lots of tender loving care at this magnificent place. Step inside and bask in the mesmerizing sounds of this nation's incredible musical history.

Paradise Records | Chengdu

What?	House, techno, disco, world sounds, and ambient recordings
Where?	Renminnanlu 49, Manhattan Building 12–8, Chengdu, China
When?	2017
Why?	One of the few contemporary record stores in China and, hopefully, the first of many

ABOVE
33 Studios is the home of Paradise Records.

The evolution of China as a global player increasingly willing to adopt Western ideas has created a new generation of young people who are more switched on than previous ones. This has had positive implications for the country's music scene, with a large degree of growth over the last couple of decades and, in particular, the rise of club and festival culture. Paradise Records is undoubtedly one of the products of this increasingly creative and fertile movement in China and a sure sign that the nation is steadily becoming a place where contemporary arts can really flourish.

Marco Duits is the mastermind behind the shop, which is very small and still in its infancy as a vinyl vendor. The Dutchman settled in Chengdu while traveling in 2001 and started doing parties in 2002. A DJ since the late 1990s, Marco channeled his love of records into promoting events in the city, nurturing a local scene that led to the opening of his own club .TAG in 2014. Paradise Records slowly evolved out of random free street parties where Marco would play vinyl with a tropical vibe during the summertime in Chengdu, in China's Sichuan province. Through the parties, Marco and his Paradise comrades built a following and started to pick up bookings for street parties elsewhere in the city. All the while, Marco was returning to Holland on a regular basis, bringing back new records each time and building up a big collection. In fact, over a period of 12 years, he amassed enough records to launch his own small pop-up stall, which he set up in various locations around the city, while also selling vinyl from his own home in the early stages of the brand's life. Paradise Records found a permanent base when some of Marco's friends opened a DJ studio and school called 33Studio. He moved all his equipment into a room at the space in 2017 and Paradise Records finally had a spot it could call home. Stocking a wide variety of house, techno, and disco, Marco also makes sure there's a good selection of world sounds and ambient recordings, too. As a beacon for the progression of China's music scene, Paradise Records is an important hub and one that will hopefully continue to push things forward both locally and internationally.

ZudRangMa Records | Bangkok

What?	**Thai funk, Luk Thung, Molam, Ethiopian pop, and a smattering of niche world music**
Where?	**51 Sukhumvit Road, Khwaeng Khlong Tan Nuea, Khet Watthana, Krung Thep Maha Nakhon 10110, Thailand**
When?	**2007**
Why?	**To discover tons of new music from Thailand and the rest of the world**

One of Bangkok's premier record stores, ZudRangMa Records is one of the cogs in a musical machine spearheaded by local DJ and music business wizard, Nat Siangsukon (aka DJ Maft Sai). As a selector and collector, Maft Sai is tenacious, passionate, and open-minded, scouring the globe for the kind of music that's completely neglected by the mainstream: Ethiopian pop, Middle Eastern funk, and a ton of Thai recordings, new and old. In fact, ZudRangMa doubles as a vital archive for Thai music, especially Thai funk, Luk Thung, and Molam— all musical styles that are intrinsic to local culture.

When you step through the doors of ZudRangMa, you enter a world of vibrant recordings from a range of artists and labels you've probably never heard of, unless you're already deeply engrossed in music from Thailand and beyond. Alongside his business partner, Chris Menist, Maft Sai has nurtured an exceptional and unique space, which is cozy, welcoming, and full of great music. Together they have also masterminded a record label and a live act (the Paradise Bangkok Molam International Band). The record label reissues rare Thai cuts, mostly Isan and Molam styles, with their other label, Paradise Bangkok, pushing out more dance floor-orientated music. Meanwhile, the Paradise Bangkok Molam International Band features Menist on drums, Maft Sai on percussion, Sawai Kaewsombat on the khaen (a harmonica-esque instrument made from bamboo), and Kammao Perdtanon who plays the traditional lute. In 2014, the band released a debut LP, *21st Century Molam*, to widespread acclaim. They have been booked to perform at Glastonbury, Field Day, Worldwide Festival, Paleo, Clandestine, and Cafe Oto in Hackney, East London. Their second LP, *Planet Lam*, was released in October 2016, to yet more critical praise. International recognition has come through a number of sources: the band was featured on Boiler Room back in September 2016; Maft Sai was a special guest at a Boiler Room session organized by Four Tet; Menist has a monthly slot on the influential online radio station NTS; and Gilles Peterson is a big supporter of their music.

Down the road, Chris and Nat's other business, the lively Studio Lam bar, operates as a great accompaniment to the record shop, showcasing a lot of the music and artists that are stocked there. A myriad local acts, such as Kammao Pertanon, Siang Hong Lion, Yaan, and Electric Phipet Band, as well as international names like Kirk Degiorgio, Andrew Ashong, Awesome Tapes From Africa, and Hugo Mendez, have all made appearances for the open-minded folk on Studio Lam's dance floor. One of the key nights there is called Isan Dancehall, with Maft Sai's expert curation delivering an exciting blend of Thai sound-system music. Chris and Nat also compiled two editions of "Sound of Siam" for Soundway Recordings, while Chris is also responsible for writing the book *Black Fire! New Spirits!* with Soul Jazz Records—the label connected to the London-based record store, Sounds of the Universe (see page 17). Both men work tirelessly to promote and nurture Thai music in all its forms, and ZudRangMa is at the core of their activities, providing the record-buying public with an unparalleled archive of the nation's rich and diverse musical heritage.

ABOVE
ZudRangMa Records and the people behind it have helped raise international awareness of Thai music and bring it to a wider audience.

LEFT
The Technics 1200, an ever-present workhorse in record stores from Bangkok to Barcelona.

RIGHT AND OPPOSITE
Tucked away inside the Kapo Factory building (opposite), you won't stumble across Red Point, but those in the know who find their way in will be greeted by an insane array of music from the Southeast Asian region.

Red Point Records Warehouse | Singapore

What?	**Music from the Far East**
Where?	**Kapo Factory Building, Blk B #06–11, 80 Playfair Road, Singapore 367998**
When?	**2000**
Why?	**You won't find a bigger or better collection of Oriental music anywhere else on Earth**

A trip down memory lane for many local customers, especially those from older generations, Red Point Records is a sprawling warehouse full to the brim with a record collection that mainly comprises music with a distinctly Eastern flavor. Opened at the dawn of the millennium in the year 2000 by its proprietor, the man himself Mr Ong, this is a very special place indeed. It's safe to say that this old building full of colorful vinyl is one of the world's greatest collections of recordings from the region in and around the Far East. Ong's personal mission is to share this prized local music from Singapore and Asia with his friends from other countries whenever they visit

his store. You'll hear a wide range of different languages—Mandarin, Hokkien, Cantonese, Tamil, Hindi, Japanese, Malay, Thai, Filipino, and many others—on a vast selection of records that represent an exhaustive list of genres, including Asian disco, soul, and funk through to Bollywood soundtracks and styles that originated in Asia, such as a-go-go, shidaiqu (Chinese folk/European jazz fusion), and xinyao (songs composed by Singaporeans about their life within the country). The collection totals around 10,000 records, stored in 2,000 square feet (186 square meters) of space.

Mr Ong can be found at the counter whenever Red Point is open, and his wife now offers a helping hand at the warehouse, coming on board four years ago after putting in a ton of work behind the scenes helping to clean the records ready for sale. Red Point is housed on the sixth floor of an unassuming building—be aware that two blocks are served by the lifts, and Red Point is in Block B. The shop can be a bit difficult to find, which makes it even more enticing and rewarding when you do eventually find that brown metal door with records stuck to it. It's a massive, well-lit place that feels very much like a big storage space, rather than a proper shop—though the music being pumped through the internal sound system and Ong's chirpy presence certainly counteract the slightly sterile esthetics. All the records are carefully labeled and organized in a way that won't stress you out. As well as the Far Eastern delights, there's lots of Western music and other genres from around the globe. Red Point's extraordinary mass of vinyl pressings is out of this world. Set a day aside and pay Ong a visit—your mind will be blown.

ASIA AND AUSTRALASIA

Hear Records | Singapore

What? **Local and international releases, both fresh and secondhand**

Where? **175B Bencoolen Street, Singapore 189651**

When? **2013**

Why? **A hub for Singapore's vinyl-collecting community**

Founded in 2013, Hear Records is promoted as a "music lifestyle retailer" and touted as Singapore's one-stop shop for vinyl enthusiasts. With two branches, Hear Records is a key player in the country's vinyl-vending game and offers a wide variety of genres, ranging from rock and pop to metal, punk, and alternative, indie through to jazz, soul, funk, and world music. The varied stock of vinyl includes over 10,000 used records and 5,000 new ones, plus they also supply turntables, audio equipment, and vinyl accessories such as record bags, slipmats, and lots more. The owner Nick Tan has transposed his experiences with record stores into his own repositories. He's a lifelong customer of the famous Foo Leong outlet in Chinatown (where the second incarnation of Hear Records opened in October 2016). Owned by Mrs Wong, a local woman in her late seventies, Foo Leong has been around since the mid-1970s. Nick's shop is very different to Mrs Wong's setup, but the inspiration lies in being able to grow a community around music in its physical form, creating a place where people can socialize and hide away from the outside world.

Some staff members only work one day a week, taking a break from their everyday jobs to do so. Nick refers to the store as an asylum—it's a place where you can escape, into music and into yourself. Hear Records has a commitment, which they call "Weekly Fresh," whereby at least one or two new vinyl shipments come through the door every week—quite rare for most vinyl stores in Asia. This policy gives customers a newly updated stock to riffle through at least once a week, which encourages them to return more often than they might do to other outlets. If that's not impressive enough, the store also imports up to 3,000 used records every six weeks or so—all handpicked and well curated.

The staff at Hear Records are all involved in the local music scene, from DJs to members of bands (such as Typewriter, Livonia, The Great Spy Experiment, Shelves, I Am David Sparkle) to gig promoters and label owners. These are people who live and breathe music, and put just as much passion into helping others learn about new artists as they do into their own musical endeavors. Nick takes pride in the store's "Support Local Support Charity" program, which involves the purchase of vinyl and CDs wholesale from local indie artists in order to support them. These releases are then sold at Hear, with 100 percent of the profits being donated to charities that work with children in need. A relatively young, yet highly influential and inspiring location that should be high up on your hit list if you're visiting Singapore.

BELOW
Be prepared to lose a few hours digging in Hear.

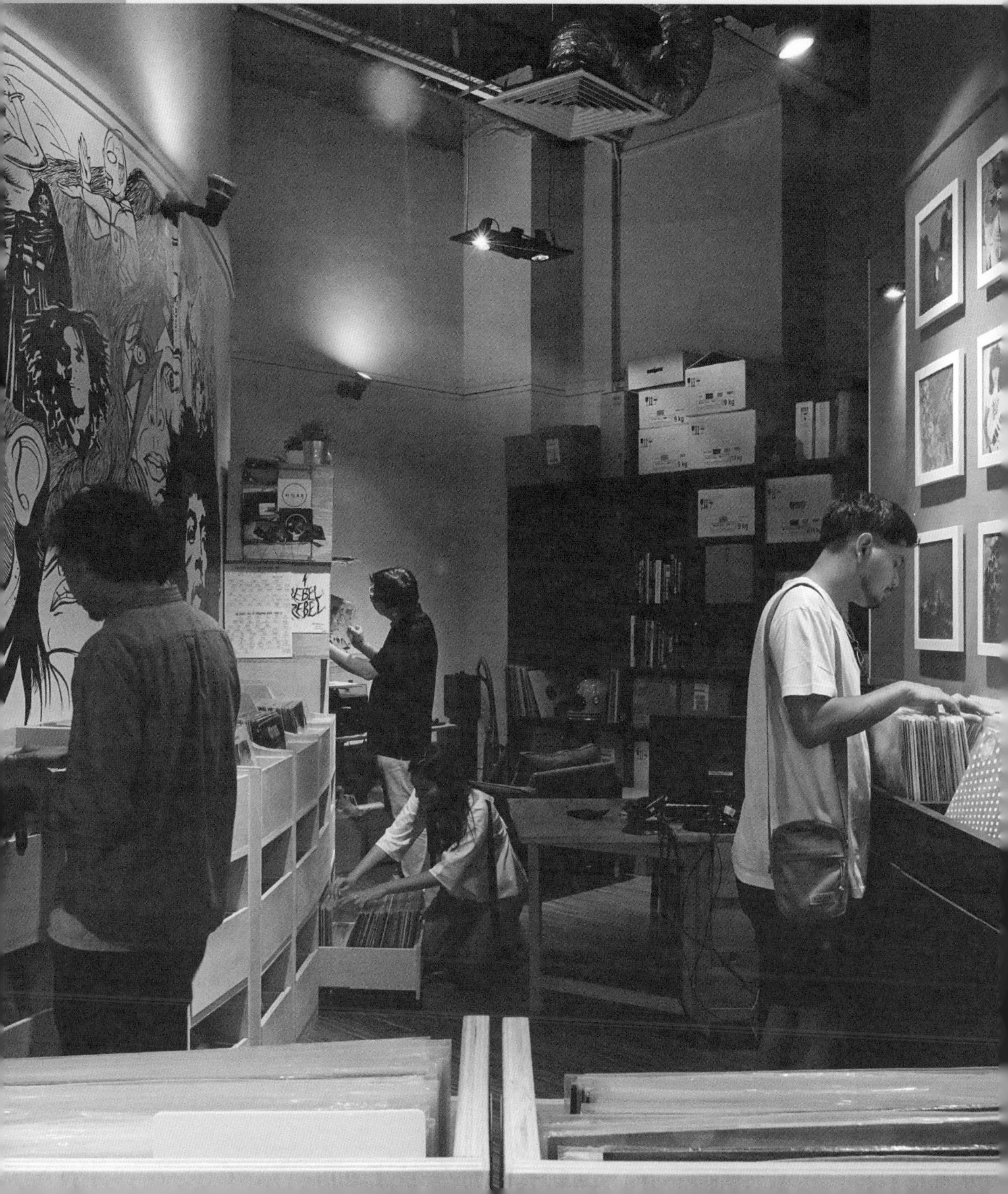

Disk Union Shinjuku | Tokyo

What?	Everything, organized with precision
Where?	Yamada Building, 3–31–4 Shinjuku, Shinjuku-ku, Tokyo 160–0022, Japan
When?	1969
Why?	A huge and amazingly well-organized place of wonder

This record-store chain has a ton of locations dotted around Japan, with its three biggest outposts in Ikebukuro, Shinjuku, and Shibuya. The most enormous is the flagship venue in Shinjuku. This absolute beast of a store is spread across eight floors, yes, EIGHT. Though each floor may be on the small side, eight floors are still eight floors. On each of the floors you'll find a different area of music covered, from punk and hardcore on the seventh floor to prog rock on the third floor and Japanese rock and pop in the basement. Hunting for vinyl at Disk Union is an intensive process but, thanks to Japanese ingenuity and thorough organization, it's not that much of a headache. Phew!

The curation and maintenance of the many outlets operating under the Disk Union umbrella are impeccable. In fact, you won't find a better-organized chain of record stores anywhere else on the planet; they even go so far as to break down punk into its various subgenres. This amplifies the shopping experience immeasurably. There is a meditative aspect to vinyl-digging, which occurs when you're way down the rabbit hole, fingers flicking on autopilot, retinas relaying information back to your brain, and mind focused solely on finding gold, black gold. A process such as this can be enhanced by the kind of smoothness and flow offered by organized shelves like those at Disk Union. On top of that, the shop's prices are competitive—often equal to, if not cheaper than, what you will find online—and they are always putting stuff on sale to clear unsold stock. Half the sales made at Disk Union come via their used section, and the shop makes billions every year. It's fair to say they are the No.1 vinyl vendor in Japan, just based on size and coverage alone. So popular is this place that even the staff from other record stores go digging there when they're not at work. If you want to have a life-affirming digging experience, you can't go wrong with Disk Union—it's a legendary chain.

Technique Records | Tokyo

What?	**Finest quality electronic music**
Where?	**33–14 Udagawa-machi Kubo Building 2F, Shibuya, Tokyo, 150–1002, Japan**
When?	**1996**
Why?	**Tokyo's best dance music supplier bar none**

If dance music is your bag, then there aren't many places in Japan that can compare with Technique Records. Specialists in club and electronic music since 1996, the shop has built a sterling reputation across Japan and the rest of the world, thanks to its dedication to giving customers the finest quality; that applies to everything, including the level of service, the music on offer, the curation, the organization of the store itself, and the equipment used in-store for listening purposes. CEO Yoshiharu Sato and his partner-in-crime, Keisuke Hirai, are the duo behind the shop, which started out as a mail-order service back in the mid-1990s. After four years, they opened a physical store due to increasing demand from their community of DJ customers and vinyl collectors. Since then, Technique has become firmly established as a reputable source of all things electronic-based, with stock ranging from deep house through to dubstep and DnB.

ABOVE
Tokyo boasts some of the best record stores in the world, and Technique leads the way when it comes to dance music.

The interior of Technique is clean, as you might expect from a Japanese establishment, with signed record sleeves, featuring messages from a wide range of influential underground heroes such as Floating Points and Move D, adorning the walls. The Chemical Brothers have been regular visitors over the years and a long list of other famous artists have passed through the shop since it first opened, keen to delve into its hefty selection of quality vinyl. The records are divided up according to genre and often include artists' names to make your hunting even easier. Technique's owners also run Energy Flash Distribution, which supports independent labels from across Japan, helping to push the scene onto the world stage and keep it buoyant. Oddly, it has to get all its releases pressed in Europe because there is no longer anywhere to manufacture vinyl in Japan. Despite the country's fascination with the CD format, Technique continues to succeed, finding its niche and really owning the electronic music space in Toyko. Of course, being connected to the local scene has been intrinsic to sustaining the store's popularity, while the distribution wing also means it is not only reliant on selling records. Slightly off the beaten path, it's well worth taking some time out to find Technique Records and immersing yourself in its impeccable collection of music.

Tower Records | Tokyo

What?	**Everything and more**
Where?	**1 Chome-22–14 Jinnan, Shibuya, Tokyo 150–0041, Japan**
When?	**1995**
Why?	**A gigantic playground for record enthusiasts and music-lovers**

A name synonymous with music retail, the Japanese branch of Tower Records is one of the very few stores still in operation. Tower Records first entered the Japanese market in 1979 with a Sapporo branch opening in 1980 and the big one, in tourist hub Shibuya, opening in 1995. Twenty one years later, the store became an independent entity when it was bought outright by the management; this meant that when the Tower Records corporation went bust in 2006, the iconic Tokyo-based outlet was unaffected and continued to operate. Japan has long been an essential destination for record fiends from all over the planet, thanks to the huge number of shops that once existed there, especially in the capital, Tokyo. It's also due to the fact that the Japanese are virtuosos when it comes to collecting, archiving, and organizing vinyl—plus record companies would often release special Japanese editions of their most sought-after LPs.

Tower Records has been one of the main digging sites for waves of vinyl enthusiasts over the last few decades, thanks to its overwhelming size and the plentiful supply of music it stocks across nine floors. Occupying over 53,820 square feet (5,000 square meters), Tower Records has a huge yellow and red sign outside the main entrance with the slogan, "No Music, No Life," which says it all really. Now, the vinyl offering there isn't as extensive as its competitors, but this is a spot where the shopping experience is so unforgettable that you can easily forgive the small number of records on offer. (If you want CDs, though, it's overrun with them, as they are still the biggest-selling format in Japan.) For such a big place, there is so much character and personality on every floor—the staff are incredibly attentive, and like to get creative

with the store's presentation, so you cannot fail to enjoy the entire experience of being inside Tower Records Japan. It's a location where pure, unadulterated love for music is evident from top to bottom.

Live performances, with a professional stage setup and a slick sound system, take place in the basement, while each of the floors above is dedicated to a different genre. Plus, there's a café on the second floor if you want to hydrate yourself during an epic digging mission. As well as the landmark store, TRJ also run their own subsidiary label, T-Palette Records, where you'll find music from the country's Japan Idol performers, plus they publish three free magazines called *Tower*, *Intoxicate*, and *Bounce*. All the music for sale is brand new; there's nothing used there—but the range (from J-pop to soul and rock) is more than adequate. Fans can attend "meet-and-greet" events, or handshakes as they're called, where their favorite stars appear in-store to meet fans, sign records, and perform. In 1996 the late, great King of Pop Michael Jackson made an appearance—of course, the entire street outside was mobbed. Michael happily met fans and also immortalized his handprints in concrete during the event. Tower also sells tons of merchandise and accessories for fans who like to collect memorabilia, from key rings and badges to personalized folders and T-shirts, as standard, plus a whole library of books and magazines. Literally a towering pillar that stands for supporting and sharing new music and one that has remained true to its ethos since the 1980s, Tower Records Japan is a legendary spot.

ASIA AND AUSTRALASIA

LEFT
50,000 square feet dedicated to music.
How could any music lover resist?

Australia and New Zealand

Red Eye Records | Sydney

What?	**Across the board, from rock to jazz and folk**
Where?	**143 York Street, Sydney, New South Wales 2000, Australia**
When?	**1981**
Why?	**It's Australia's biggest independent record store**

As soon as you step off York Street, behind the huge landmark that is the Queen Victoria Building in Sydney's Central Business District, and make your way into Red Eye Records, you're greeted with the bright red walls of one of the city's vinyl institutions. The bold color sets the shop apart from many of its counterparts around the globe, and gives it a unique visual identity that is, of course, inspired by its name.

Set up by Chris Pepperell, Red Eye is Australia's largest independent record store and the winner of two ARIA (Australian Recording Industry Association) Awards for "Best Independent Physical Retailer In Australia." Chris got involved in selling records back in the 1960s as a way of making money to buy more records of his own. After landing a job at Anthem Records in the early 1970s, Chris spent a decade learning the trade firsthand before moving on to start Red Eye in 1981. With that many miles on the clock, you know you're in for a smooth ride with this awesome place. Slink down the stairs, past a few glass displays featuring some of the many box sets and LPs for sale, and you end up in the main basement space, where the walls and store floor are lined with shelves full of black wax, CDs, and DVDs. A beneficiary of the global upsurge in physical sales—according to ARIA figures, vinyl sales doubled in 2014, increasing by a staggering 127 percent, with continuous growth year on year since then—Red Eye is doing better than ever nowadays, outlasting the eight or so other independent retailers that were located in Sydney's CBD when it opened.

The shop's premise is simple and hasn't changed since it first opened; it sells good-quality music in a traditional record-store environment—for many, this conjures up feelings of nostalgia, which adds to their shopping experience. There's nothing fancy, no pretence or superficiality, just a very good vinyl outlet that has honed its craft with lots of love, care, and attention since its inception. The staff are keen to help with anything and everything; the records are carefully curated to offer the best to a wide demographic of music-lovers; and the prices are pretty reasonable, though sometimes at the higher end of the spectrum. However, you get what you pay for, and operating in such a central location is not cheap. In the great tradition of record stores, some of the staff members have been working there since they were in their teens, including the manager, Matt, and Chris' business partner, Adam, for example, who both started at Red Eye as work-experience boys at the age of 15. Like Matt, Adam, and many of the shop's long-term customers, once you visit Red Eye Records you'll become a lifelong devotee, so make sure you swing by if you're in Sydney.

Rocking Horse | Brisbane

What?	**Copious amounts of vinyl, plus tickets and merch**
Where?	**Queen Street Mall, 245 Albert Street, Brisbane City, Queensland 4000, Australia**
When?	**1975**
Why?	**To experience a place that's been reppin' strong for a very long time**

If you see a queue of people snaking down from Queen Street Mall in Brisbane's Central Business District, then it's more than likely they're waiting to buy tickets from Queensland's oldest and largest record store, Rocking Horse. Besides its copious stock of vinyl, this seminal spot also sells tickets for many of Brisbane's big concerts, which often leads eager fans to form long lines that extend beyond the exit and out into the street. Of course, the main draw is the extensive selection of records—name a genre and they will most likely have it on the shelves. If not, you can always make a polite request and staff will do their best to order it in, or point you in the right direction so you can track it down. Rocking Horse is the kind of place that, like many of its cousins around the globe, has amassed a strong and loyal community of music fanatics who all devote a large percentage of their time to hunting down records to add to their collections. So engaged is their following that, in 2011, when the store came under threat of closure, over 7,000 people committed to attending an event organized to save it.

Overwhelming local support is undoubtedly part of the reason that the shop survived and still exists today. There is no accounting for the influence that a vinyl outlet has on its local community, from simply providing a space for people to congregate and socialize, to keeping the local music scene energized; they are an essential feature of many cities on every one of the planet's continents. Rocking Horse has been intrinsic to Brisbane's record-collecting community since 1975, so, of course, its influence filters down through several generations. Owner Warwick Vere moved north to Brisbane from his native Sydney in the early 1970s and managed to catch a wave, starting Rocking Horse purely as a hobby. Over the years, the store has become his lifeblood, a place where he can channel his undying passion for records and one that has become his second home—it is a physical manifestation of the love he has for music. On Valentine's Day, 1989, Rocking Horse was targeted by a Government crackdown on "obscene" recordings and raided by police. A myriad naughty pressings were cited as examples of the obscenity that the Government was trying to eradicate, presumably in the name of protecting the country's youth from being corrupted—among them were The Dead Kennedys' *Give Me Convenience* (featuring "Too Drunk To F***"), The Champs' "Do The Shag," and *Dickcheese* by the Hard-Ons. Weathering those storms makes Rocking Horse even more legendary (Warwick won the case, by the way), and it's a living embodiment of the ever-present power of counterculture.

Running a record shop for over 40 years means Warwick has been privy to how the many changes in society affect record shoppers. For instance, he says there is now an equal balance between the genders of his customers, which was never the case back in 1975. With the ongoing conversation over patriarchy and misogyny, it's encouraging to know that women make up such a large percentage of the people who visit his store. Of course, everyone is welcomed with open arms at Rocking Horse, and its inclusive atmosphere, combined with its history, connection with customers and the local community, and progressive attitude, makes it a unique place to shop.

ASIA AND AUSTRALASIA

The Record Exchange | Brisbane

What?	**Over 200,000 records, so a bit of everything**
Where?	**1/65 Adelaide Street, Brisbane City, Queensland 4000, Australia**
When?	**Unknown**
Why?	**Lose a few hours rummaging through the chaotic assortment of records**

Home to well over 200,000 records, The Record Exchange touts itself as Australia's biggest record store. With huge premises on Adelaide Street in the center of Brisbane (and not far from Rocking Horse Records, see page 101), it's a crucial destination for ardent record archeologists and those who just want to while away an afternoon perusing the racks. When you walk into The Record Exchange, one thing you'll notice immediately is that it's a little bit of a mess. For the more Feng Shui-orientated shopper, this may prove a bit of a headache; however, if you're patient and are less precious about organization, then you'll be fine. The clutter is part of the store's charm, so be prepared. It can take a while to find what you're looking for, but you'll probably unearth a few unexpected treats along the way, which is always an exciting part of the digging process. Like a paleontologist, you may even excavate a few surprise fossils while delving into the mountains of records on display.

Owner Richard Hart is a veteran of the record-store game, with a CV that dates back to the 1970s. In that time, he has owned several vinyl boutiques, including a spot on the infamous Hollywood Boulevard. His deep love for collecting music has led to 40-plus years of involvement in buying and selling records. When you visit his store, all that experience is at your disposal, together with an expansive selection of music and memorabilia. At The Record Exchange there's every chance you will lose the best part of a day trawling through all the music—in fact, it's inevitable. But what better way to let a few hours slip by?

Wax Museum Records | Melbourne

What?	**Alternative, hip hop, and electronic through to soul, jazz, and weirdness**
Where?	**Shop 2, Campbell Arcade, Degraves Street (Flinders Street Subway), Melbourne, Victoria 3000, Australia**
When?	**2006**
Why?	**A firsthand insight into the Melbourne music scene**

With its clever name, Wax Museum is a place that you won't forget in a hurry. Based in Melbourne, it is one of several key vinyl vendors in the city and is flourishing despite the healthy competition. The vinyl revival everyone has been talking about for the past few years has well and truly hit Melbourne, a city where a large majority of the inhabitants are young, upwardly mobile, and switched on to the latest global trends. Hipster culture, start-ups aplenty, and a vibrant music scene mean record sales are strong, and Wax Museum caters for those who love the more alternative side of music—think hip hop and future beats with a smattering of house, techno, boogie, disco, and lots more, including more left-field cuts such as audio art, anime soundtracks, and ambient studies.

The store opened in 2006 with co-owners Tim Bartold (aka DJ Aux One) and Michael O'Donnell (Mixa) adding a good dose of spit and polish to their small corner of the Campbell Arcade to create a record-buyer's haven. Taking inspiration from the quaint Japanese model, they decked the interior out in polished concrete and raw wood, setting up a space where the digging experience is complemented by the plush surroundings. The shop is cozy and has clearly had a lot of love poured into it. The walls are adorned with posters, flyers, and record album covers,

RIGHT
As the shop's logo suggests, it's all about the beats at the Wax Museum.

plus a few neatly arranged shelves. All the staff members are DJs, producers, and promoters who are actively involved in the local music community—the roster includes Benny Badge (owner of Gulf Point Records), DJ Mindtwist of Sleep D (and owner of Butter Sessions), and Barry Sunset of Spin Club. They will happily impart their knowledge of the records on sale, interesting artists and labels, and the Melbourne scene, of course. In fact, if you want firsthand insight on what's happening in Melbs, then this is the team you need to consult. The store also lends its name to a label run by Aux One and Guy Roseby, which focuses on releasing interesting local music, including Plutonic Lab, local boogie band Silver Linings, side projects by Horatio Luna and Ziggy Zeitgeist of 30/70, and Sydney's DJ Soup. Quirky, connected, and universally acclaimed, Wax Museum is the tiny giant of the Melbourne scene.

Real Groovy | Auckland

What?	**Music of all kinds, comics, oddities, and pop memorabilia**
Where?	**369 Queen Street, Auckland 1010, New Zealand**
When?	**1981**
Why?	**A huge place of worship for all music disciples**

When a record vendor goes beyond the standard formula to bring something else to the table, you know you're in good hands. Real Groovy has a few extras up its sleeve that make it an absolute pleasure to visit. Tucked away in New Zealand's largest urban conurbation, it feels like a retreat, a sanctuary away from the din of the city. Set up way back in 1981 by Chris Hart and Chris Priestly, it is a behemoth, dwarfing most record-pressing plants, let alone stores. Due to its history, size, and ridiculous range of music and gifts, Real Groovy has a global fan base and an unsurpassed reputation.

It hasn't been a smooth path for the beloved Kiwi spot—in 2008 the owners were on the brink of closing it down, due to a downfall in sales brought on by the global recession and a dwindling interest in vinyl. In 2017, they had to abandon their famous premises on Queen Street, leaving behind years and years of history and memories, to transfer the business just across the street to an old Salvation Army church. Unsurprisingly, the unstoppable machine that is the property market had a large part to play in this relocation, with the old building they occupied being demolished to make way for... yep, you guessed it, apartments. Still, you can never be overly sentimental in the record-store business, and they've taken the move on the chin, continuing to sell their wares with aplomb and making full use of the new space—even retaining the altar. In fact, since the exterior still has a "holy" feel, the new space could be considered a place of worship for all devotees of the acetate God that we call Vinyl-mighty.

At Real Groovy, you not only get a huge selection of new and secondhand records, but are also blessed with comics, nerdy gifts, and a whole host of other off-the-wall products. The shop also stocks turntables and audio equipment, answering the prayers of music enthusiasts and anyone else who wants to track down a unique gift. The basement, where all the records are kept, is massive, with records hanging from the ceiling and long rows of boxes and racks full of vinyl from all the way back to the classical era right up to today's pop and rap superstars. Before you know it, you've spent half a day immersed in the never-ending array of stock. All the staff are music lifers, which means they are dedicated to providing the best service possible—not

because they are trained to sell, sell, sell, but because they love music and want to share it with people, to inform people about its history, and to make the whole record-shopping experience a pleasurable one. So, there's no chance of encountering a miserable clerk behind the counter. It's all smiles and good vibes at Real Groovy, a sacred space that is way up there on the list of the world's biggest and best record stores and where real-life miracles can happen.

BELOW
Real Groovy is a stalwart in the New Zealand music world.
Not only is it one of the country's oldest record shops, it
is also home to one of its largest selections of vinyl.

ABOVE
Waterloo Records,
Austin

Chapter Five

North America

5

BELOW
Electric Fetus, Minneapolis

United States

Amoeba Music | Los Angeles

What?	**Everything**
Where?	**6400 Sunset Boulevard, Los Angeles, CA 90028, USA**
When?	**1997**
Why?	**In this case, size matters**

Whether you're a dedicated follower of all things vinyl, or simply fancy spending a day trawling through thousands of records, Amoeba is THE place to go. The biggest of three California-based record stores, Amoeba takes up almost an entire block on Sunset Boulevard in LA; its sheer size (24,000 square feet/2,230 square meters) makes it an essential destination, as it can house over 250,000 records. Of course, under such a large roof, you will find a comprehensive array of genres and artists from as far back as Louis Armstrong's era and beyond. It's a treasure trove, a super-sized warehouse where you can really lose yourself perusing the stacks and stacks of vinyl. In fact, a day may not be enough—and don't forget there are two more branches of Amoeba: the original on Telegraph Avenue, Berkeley, and another on Haight Street, in San Francisco.

Amoeba is one of the most famous record shops on the planet and upholds an ethos dedicated to the preservation and sale of high-quality music in physical format. The team behind the store live for music; some of them are musicians themselves, and it's their passion for the art form that makes Amoeba such a special place. Owners Dave Prinz, Karen Pearson, Marc Weinstein, and Jim Henderson

ABOVE
One of, if not the largest independent music store in the world. That's all you need to know.

have created a heavenly space whose size is matched by the quality and depth of the music collection. Expert curation doesn't get any better than this. To amass such a huge amount of good music, where the quality very rarely dips, is no mean feat, and record collectors the world over will vouch for the amazing selection at Amoeba.

NORTH AMERICA

The second you step through the doors, you are whisked away to another dimension, where all that exists is the magic of frequency recorded to wax by some of the world's greats, new and old. Like many of the most famous large record shops, Amoeba has also become a live music spot, where artists pass through to perform and sign their latest releases, thus adding to its already immense appeal. If you want to enter a dreamworld, where the only thing that exists is music, then this is the only place to go.

Mississippi Records | Portland

What?	**Left-of-center, rare, and challenging releases from all over the world**
Where?	**5202 North Albina Avenue, Portland, Oregon 97217, USA**
When?	**2003**
Why?	**For an intimate shopping experience, with records you won't find anywhere else for miles**

First things first, Mississippi Records isn't located in Mississippi. In fact, it is about 2,500 miles (4,000km) from the place it's named after. Secondly, the store has very little Internet presence, mainly because owner Eric Isaacson has no interest in the online world. Yep, hard to quantify for those of us who are firmly hardwired into digital life, but Eric finds it "boring" and has no interest in being a part of it... or having a mobile phone either. What a breath of fresh air. This attitude feeds back into his record shop (and also its label offshoot), which has established itself as a prime source of alternative music and the kind of releases that you probably won't find anywhere else in Oregon, if not the rest of America. The storefront is white and pale blue, with a traditional-style font displaying the shop's name above the door. Inside, everything is pretty much par for the course, with well-organized boxes of records filling most of the store floor, but with a decent amount of space for navigating the remaining floor space, even when it's busy. The genre dividers are blessed with a rather artistic touch, while the owner's dogs can usually be found hanging out among the records too, giving it a very homely feel. The selection isn't huge, but what's there is absolute gold, and the vinyl is accompanied by a sizeable selection of cassette tapes, which are very hard to find these days.

Since launching in 2003 Mississippi Records has maintained a fiercely independent outlook, putting its energy into creating a space where people can connect through music. Its ethos centers on viewing physical music as more than a mere commodity, but rather as a means to connect, grow spiritually, and embellish one's life in a myriad ways. The label wing started when one of the staff members wanted to put out a debut album, but couldn't find a home for it. Mississippi Records was set up to help get his music out there, and now, well over 200 releases later, it is recognized as a key source of alternative music by collectors and distributors all over the world. Eric teamed up with long-time friend Warren Hill to work on the label, putting their minds together to create a platform where local and international musicians sit side by side, and a slew of interesting, often challenging, new music has been released as a result. In-store gigs are not uncommon and collectors travel from all over the globe to spend time at the shop. Eric does his utmost to keep prices reasonable, so as not to alienate potential customers and to be as egalitarian as possible. In its hometown of Portland, where many of America's more alternative-minded residents are based, Mississippi Records stands for equal rights, inclusiveness, and the power of music to unite and affect change. A beacon of hope in the era of Trump.

Forever Young Records | Grand Prairie

What?	**Everything and more**
Where?	**2955 TX-360, Grand Prairie, Texas 75052, USA**
When?	**1984**
Why?	**It's big, yet welcoming, and full of treasure**

You might need to book yourself a few days away from the world if you really want to get stuck into a full-on digging session at Forever Young, as this place is absolutely huge. Owner David Eckstrom started out as a collector (surprise, surprise) and seller at the local Texan flea market Traders Village in 1981. Three years later and he'd set up the first Forever Young in Irving, with a second premises following in Arlington in 1989. But the biggie was born in 1998 when he managed to purchase a whole acre of land off Highway 360, where he built the behemoth that is the current Forever Young. This spot takes up 11,500 square feet (1,068 square meters) of retail floor space and contains over 250,000 records.

As you might expect in a store of such magnitude, there is a breathtaking array of different musical styles from all eras, with lots of special items, collectables, limited-edition presses, bargains, merchandise, and much more. David runs the shop with his wife, Patricia, and their children, Taylor Eckstrom and Tavia Muzzi, plus music-buyer Ed Swiencki. Walking in through the main doors, you'll be immediately excited and overwhelmed by the gargantuan store and its range of music, which is beyond extensive. Take a deep breath, and perhaps do some pre-shopping groundwork to think about what you want to find (and maybe even take a list with you) if you're serious about buying something particular and want to avoid feeling intimidated—even if you wish to browse at your leisure, this may also help you stay focused if you're worried about getting lost. If you're happy to lose yourself, then this is most definitely the place to do it. David and his team will happily guide you through your shopping experience if you need assistance—they are always there for you to lean on.

Forever Young is laid out in long rows of shelf units and boxes, with the music painstakingly arranged according to genre, era, and so forth. It is a testament to the Forever Young family that their sprawling store is kept in such good order. Shopping for records there is a truly unique experience that you won't get in many other places on the planet. Those seeking out rare cuts also have their own spot, the Record Collectors' Den,

where you can find records valued upward of $75, plus glass cases displaying hard-to-get-old-of memorabilia. An incredible shop with depth, history, and character and so many records that you'll need a few days to search through them all. Heaven on Earth.

LEFT
Used cassettes, 45s, old hi-fi equipment, eight-tracks, reel-to-reel recorders, turntables, T-shirts, and posters are all on sale alongside the vinyl and CDs.

NORTH AMERICA

Waterloo Records | Austin

What?	**Everything you can imagine**
Where?	**600 North Lamar Boulevard, Austin, Texas 78703, USA**
When?	**1982**
Why?	**To feel genuine, heartfelt love for music and vinyl**

Operating at the heart of Austin's music scene since 1982, Waterloo Records has a sterling reputation. In fact, you're more likely to track down a dodo in the wild than you are to meet someone who's had a bad experience there, so committed are the staff to giving each customer the same love and attention they give to their records. Louis Karp founded Waterloo, and was soon joined by John Kunz, who came in as a partner. Nowadays, Kunz is the sole owner, remaining true to the store's original outlook: love for music above all else and a fiercely independent approach that encompasses unwavering support for the local community.

Waterloo Records is built on love: love for music, love for sharing music, and love for discovering music. This approach is special when you encounter it because it's so pure and unconditional. With a good few miles on the clock, the shop has seen a lot of custom come through its hallowed doors, which means their level of customer service is high. In fact, one of their key policies is "customers first"—a failsafe way to achieve success, especially if you measure success by how many people leave with a smile on their face. Wareloo has also been a popular destination for many local and international artists.

As well as row upon row of crates and boxes full of records, all loving labeled and arranged by the staff, the store is also a great hangout spot. People can actually spend good-quality time with one another there, an experience that is becoming increasingly rare in our fast-paced world. Friendships are formed and collaborative projects spring forth from some of the connections made between musicians there. There are regular in-store gigs, especially when Austin's world-famous South By Southwest music conference is on. For a few weeks, the whole city is overrun with bands, singers, rappers, DJs, and a plethora of music-industry heads—lawyers, managers, label heads, agents, and so on—and there are gigs taking place anywhere and everywhere you can imagine. Waterloo Records has hosted hundreds of shows over the years, with a long, long list of famous faces performing there, including The Stooges, Sonic Youth, Jeff Buckley, Queens of the Stone Age, My Bloody Valentine, Norah Jones, and many others. They also organize in-store signings, where fans can meet their idols and get their CD or vinyl signed.

Waterloo's interior is big (6,400 square feet/600 square meters to be exact), so you'll need to allocate a good amount of time if you're serious about embarking on a dig there. The shelves are arranged neatly, with clear labeling across all sections. There's a section labeled with days of the week, so you can select records based on when they arrived in stock; staff picks play over the internal speakers; and cheaper records are close to the counters—plus, as you might expect, there are record players available for those who want to pitch up and scan through their stacks of future purchases.

ABOVE
When faced with such an eye-wateringly expansive amount of records,
your bank balance might meet its Waterloo once you enter within.

One thing that stands out above everything else is the level of service you get at Waterloo Records—the staff really imbue the store with good vibes and are attentive to everyone's needs, often going above and beyond the call of duty to ensure customers get what they need. In fact, one local couple felt so connected to the vinyl outlet that they decided to get married there. Grayson Niven and Angelica Collins said "I do" in a low-key ceremony in the aisles of the shop in November 2017. The DIY ethos of Waterloo Records has kept it relevant and intrinsically linked to a wide variety of local musicians, many of whom had their first gig at the store or met their fellow bandmates there. As Austin's music scene thrives and vinyl sales continue to surge, Waterloo Records is poised to keep spreading the love for many years to come.

LEFT
Be sure to check out the merch in store and show Euclid some love.

RIGHT
Euclid does an outstanding job of keeping the punters happy in a city where music is embedded in its cultural DNA.

Euclid Records | New Orleans

What?	**Local music, plus a whole host of global sounds**
Where?	**3301 Chartres Street, New Orleans, Louisiana 70117, USA**
When?	**2010**
Why?	**For an insight into the wonderful world of New Orleans and its unique music scene**

New Orleans is one of America's most vibrant and unique cities. So, unsurprisingly, one of its finest record stores is equally vivacious and full of boundless energy. One look at the old exterior, which was bright pink, would have alerted you to the fact that you were going to have a record-shopping experience like no other. Sadly, since Euclid moved farther down the street from the original location, it has shed the hot-pink storefront, but the interior is still full of character and, more importantly, the kind of positive, community-focused atmosphere that separates a good record shop from a great one.

Owner James Weber spent several years satiating his hunger for records at a place called Vintage Vinyl, in St. Louis, before relocating to New Orleans. Fate brought him together with Brian Bromberg, a New Yorker who was working at Peaches Records in the city. The chemistry between the two men was just right, so right, in fact, they were soon planning to get their own vinyl emporium off the ground, confident that they could do it better than anyone else. James hit up his friend Joe Schwab, owner of the original Euclid Records, and suggested that he and Brian set up a franchise of the business. In the lead-up to this, he'd been selling records at open-air markets in the locality, building a strong community around record buying, and so, when Euclid opened in the French Quarter in 2010, they already had a loyal clientele. The quirky outlet brought something new to the surrounding area, which was starved of a record store until it opened; this bolstered its credentials on opening and it was a success pretty much from the get-go. In 2014, the shop moved to its current location, due to a need for more space, and has remained an important cultural hub in the city ever since.

The interior is full of character, a unique space in a unique city. From the staircase painted to look like the keys of a piano to the exposed brick walls, from the decorative art hanging from the ceiling and the multicolored shelves holding a collection of well over 70,000 records to the staff jokes on record dividers, Euclid is one of a kind. Weber's aim has always been to establish a space where cultural exchange occurs, where people can meet, hang out, and spend time together away from the pressures of the modern world. It's a liberating space where you can form strong bonds with fellow vinyl enthusiasts, enjoy amazing live performances from local acts all through the week, and enjoy digging your way deep down into the vinyl rabbit hole. Weber and Bromberg are the architects of a musical sanctuary that really feeds the soul and offers solace from the world at large. Once you step in, make sure you switch off your phone, block out any thoughts of the outside world, and lose yourself in music for a few hours. You won't regret it.

Grimey's | Nashville

What?	**Rock 'n' roll, indie, and much more**
Where?	**1604 8th Avenue South, Nashville, Tennessee 37203, USA. Moving to a new location in late 2018: 1060 E Trinity Lane, Nashville, TN 37216, USA**
When?	**1999**
Why?	**A Nashville mainstay with a sterling rep and killer in-store performances**

Nashville is home to Americana, and a plethora of musical legends, including Billy Ray Cyrus, Kings Of Leon, Ke$ha, and more, hail from this city. It is a magnet for musicians from all over the world, thanks to its history and countless music studios. With such a strong reputation and fertile music scene, Nashville's record-store credentials are impressive, and Grimey's New & Preloved Music stands out as one of its precious gems.

Set up in December 1999 by Mike Grimes, at the time of writing the shop has two locations, Grimey's and Grimey's Too, which specializes in used records and features a bookstore called Howlin' Books and the Frothy Monkey coffee shop. However, exciting new changes are afoot. Due to the building housing Grimey's Too being sold and uncertainties regarding lease extensions at the main site, the plan is to consolidate both branches and make the move across town into a huge new site on Trinity Lane in East Nashville. Housed in a former church, the new Grimey's will offer a lot more space—over 4,000 square feet/370 square meters—for records and their famous in-store shows. Once in operation (they hope to be open by Black Friday 2018), this should see Grimey's maintaining pride of place in Nashville's musical universe, offering fans a comprehensive stock of music, slightly weighted toward rock 'n' roll.

Mike Grimes is a musician himself, having moved to the place they call "Music City" in 1989 to play in a band called Go-Go Surreal and later finding fame and fortune playing bass with The Bis-Quits (signed to John Prine's famous Oh Boy Records) and then with Bare Jr., who got together in 1998. A year later Mike quit the band and, by his own admission, had little else to do, so he set up Grimey's with his 17,000-strong record collection. He subsequently linked up with his business partner, Doyle Davis, working tirelessly to make Grimey's a haven for music-lovers, whether they want to while away their time searching for rare cuts, catch a hot new local band in action, or just want to hang out in a warm, clean, relatively quiet place. Grimey's has become one of Nashville's most beloved independent music retailers, with people traveling from far and wide to pay a visit. Managers Anna Lundy and Josh Walker keep things ticking over on the shop floor and behind the counter, while Mike and Doyle push the buttons in the control center.

Grimey's has skillfully created an atmosphere that is instantly calming; the smell of vintage acetate fills the air like incense, grounding you and sparking that inner drive to seek out some new additions

for your record collection. The store definitely has a unique vibe, but the owners are confident that the new East Nashville venue will continue to offer the same sense of character. The shop regularly hosts gigs and shows, with a few high-profile performers appearing at "off-the-radar" events over the years. These include Metallica, The Black Keys, Jason Isbell, Margo Price, Kacey Musgraves, Mumford & Sons, Phoenix, Sharon Jones & The Dap-Kings, Paramore, The Avett Brothers, Yo La Tengo, The War On Drugs, Kurt Vile, Ty Segall, and Courtney Barnett. Such is the pull of the store that it's not uncommon to bump into famous faces perusing the shelves, and you may also end up befriending a fellow shopper, as Grimey's encourages a social vibe at all times. On Saturdays, they even serve up free beer, courtesy of local breweries. There is no better representative of Nashville's Music City nickname than this wonderful shop and long may its reign continue.

Shangri-La Records | Memphis

What?	**Memphis rock 'n' roll, baby! And tons of regional and international music, plus collectibles and merch**
Where?	**1916 Madison Avenue, Memphis, Tennessee 38104, USA**
When?	**1988**
Why?	**A unique place to immerse yourself in Memphis musical history**

Set up in an early 20th-century house on Madison Avenue in the heart of midtown Memphis, Shangri-La Records specializes in Memphis-centric, regional music and collectibles. The shop is a great place to find classic favorites and catch up on what's new in the birthplace of rock 'n' roll. It dates back to 1988 when the original owner Sherman Willmott set up the magical space as a "vacation for the mind and body." The restored house, which was built in 1900, offered visitors the use of sensory-deprivation flotation tanks, as well as massages and "brain-tuners" (i.e. a set of goggles/headphones that played soothing music while flashing pulses of light around the eyes). Perhaps a little bit "ahead of its time," shall we say, Sherman's alternative endeavor soon morphed into a record store, accumulating thousands of records and becoming a spiritual space for different reasons.

At Shangri-La you get an exceptional experience, merging a unique premises with a stellar selection of records and the spellbinding history of Memphis' music scene. It's a winning combination that has captured the imagination of vinyl enthusiasts from as far afield as Japan. In fact, records aside, the shop is a local landmark simply because of the ornate nature of the building that houses it. Sherman Willmott eventually moved on in 1999 to become curator of the infamous Stax Museum of American Soul Music; at that point, Jared McStay joined Shangri-La and remains there to this day. McStay was

a member of the Simpletones, a band that released its music via the Shangri-La label. Jared and his wife, Lori, now co-own the store with John Miller, who manages the shop and is also co-owner of the Misspent Records singles label. Shangri-La has a long history of nurturing independent record labels—over the years, its numerous employees have gone on to run outlets such as Goner Records, Sugar Ditch Records, Electraphonic Recordings, and many more. Further bolstering its connection with the local community, every year Shangri-La hosts popular festivals in spring, summer, and fall, which feature local artists and huge discount sales. An unforgettable record store, Shangri-La is one of a kind; it's just a shame they don't do massages anymore.

LEFT
Memphis is a city that oozes musical history, and Shangri-La offers a bricks-and-mortar embodiment of that heritage.

Electric Fetus | Minneapolis

What?	**Everything**
Where?	**2000 4th Ave South, Minneapolis, Minnesota 55404, USA**
When?	**1968**
Why?	**A cultural icon adored by Prince and thousands more**

We may never discover the origins of the bizarre title that has been bestowed on this Minneapolis institution, but one thing is for sure, wherever it came from, Electric Fetus is a store name you won't forget in a hurry. Born in 1968, during a time when America and much of the Western world was going through a massive cultural upheaval, the early days of the Fetus (its embryonic years) are described by the shop's owners as a "cultural experiment." Partners Dan Foley and Ron Korsh got the store off the ground with $254 worth of goods, which included a bunch of psychedelic rock records.

Several months after opening, Korsh's half of the business was sold to Keith Covart who, in 1978, picked up Foley's half, too. In the era of hippies, there was a monumental change in social attitudes, particularly among younger generations, and this utopian vision was reflected in the shop. For instance, as legend has it, customers would often find the store counter empty, with a note left asking anyone to simply leave money for their haul next to the cash register. Then there were the battles with the authorities over politically themed window displays, plus the infamous Streakers Sale, where people could take as much as they could carry so long as they shopped in the nude. Nowadays, Electric Fetus is a little tamer, in that respect at least. However, the open-minded ethos remains strong, influencing the stock the store carries, which is probably the most eclectic in town. There isn't much you won't find there, and if there's something on your list they don't have, then the Fetus team will happily order it in for you.

The shop is famous for its connection to Minneapolis' most famous son, the pop legend Prince. His last-ever tweet was a link to the store's website and he had been a regular customer at Electric Fetus since the 1980s, paying his last visit a few days before he passed. The link to Prince, who sold some merchandise exclusively through the store, made Electric Fetus even more of a landmark than it already was. Business has been so good that owner Stephanie Covart Meyerring was one of the winners of the 2017 Minneapolis/St. Paul *Business Journal*'s "Women In Business Award" for steering the Fetus through a strong period of growth after she took over from her father, Keith Covart. Having said that, the owners had to shut down one of their three outlets, in St. Cloud, back in 2014. This hard but necessary decision meant they could pour more resources into bolstering the two remaining branches. Inside the main store on 4th Avenue, the space is big enough to hold 50,000 records, yet feels cozy and chilled. The team are adept at offering information on all stock, as well as nudging you in the direction of artists and labels similar to the ones you like. Live in-store gigs, tickets, merch, and a strong connection to the local music community are extra features that make this one of the best vinyl outlets in the world.

NORTH AMERICA

Dusty Groove | Chicago

What?	**A broad, eclectic selection**
Where?	**1120 North Ashland Avenue, Chicago, IL 60622, USA**
When?	**1996**
Why?	**The bargain basement alone is worth a trip, let alone the stock upstairs**

ABOVE
Dusty Groove
celebrated its
20th anniversary
in 2016.

Dusty Groove's humble beginnings go all the way back to an apartment on the south side of Chicago in 1996. Back then it operated as a mail-order service. Just over a year later, in August 1997, the business moved to a bigger space—a second-floor loft in the Wicker Park neighborhood—and only opened at weekends to begin with. Three years later, the founders, Rick Wojcik and John P Schauer (aka JP Chill), opened the physical venue at N Ashland Ave & W Haddon Ave, which is known as Ashland and Haddon to locals. From 2001, when they made the move, up until now, taking the store from its modest inception to being a globally recognized center for vinyl zealots has been a labor of love for the two men. For instance, in the early days, Wojcik, a former DJ at the University of Chicago, spent hours writing thousands of enthusiastic mini reviews of the music they were selling to give customers an insight into all the releases. This hands-on, personal touch lies at the heart of the shop's success; loving care has been injected into every aspect of Dusty Groove, which both men regard as a "conduit for other people's genius."

In the backroom, staff members pick up online orders (which still account for around 80 percent of DG's sales), pack them, and then send them off around the globe. Inside the store, with its red-brick exterior, you'll find a mass of well-organized vinyl, most of which is kept in plastic sleeves, together with a wide range of music on CD. You may find Rick or JP behind the counter, wearing one of their famous denim Dusty Groove aprons, representing the beloved shop to the fullest. Get yourself downstairs to the bargain basement, where you can pick up LPs, 12-inches, CDs, and tapes (two for $1), and 78s and 7-inches (four for $1). The selection is incredibly broad, so you're sure to find something you like, no matter what your tastes are. Interestingly, in 2012, Dusty Groove bought 50 percent of a huge archive of records from local radio station WGN. The music had been stored away in a library at the station's HQ, but was rarely used. Rick and JP put in a bid to WGN and secured half the collection, taking delivery of over 20,000 LPs, 40,000 45s, and several thousand CDs, which were all put up for sale in the shop and online. Much of the store's music comes from people who have to give up their collections for one reason or another, mostly life transitions. That's something we can sometimes forget when buying secondhand vinyl—every record has a story to tell and a history. At Dusty Groove you can delve into an endless pool of used records and try to imagine what those stories are—a compelling adventure awaits; all you have to do is step through the front door.

BELOW
Dusty Groove's stock is sourced on record-buying trips around the globe.

Reckless Records | Chicago

What?	**Rock and pop to reggae and soul**
Where?	**1379 North Milwaukee Avenue, Chicago, Illinois 60622, USA**
When?	**1988**
Why?	**To lose more than a few hours, but gain a wealth of knowledge and new music**

This Chicago institution has its roots in London, where the original Reckless Records shop opened way, way back in 1984. The Soho outlet gave birth to several offspring, and the Chicago branch, which opened in 1988, has been their most popular by a long shot. In the Windy City there are three Reckless outposts, with the North Milwaukee Avenue premises being the biggest and best-known. In 2015, they moved a couple of blocks down the road to more spacious premises, thus improving the shopping experience and giving themselves space to house even more records than they had before. According to reports, Charles Taylor, the chief executive officer of Reckless Records, bought the 100-year-old, two-storey brick building at 1379 North Milwaukee Avenue for a cool $1,580,000. Not bad, considering the location, and certainly a result for all those who venture down that avenue to get their fill of Reckless.

Musical styles of all kinds are catered for, with rock, pop, reggae, soul, jazz, and punk among some of the main genres. Staff members know what's what and won't hesitate to help you, offer some extra insight, or even push you into challenging your tastes a little, which is an admirable quality. There's a very slight air of elitism, but it comes from a good place, with no animosity or vindictiveness attached—only love and compassion. It's a big store, so be prepared to spend a lot of time getting stuck into the boxes—you will find it hard to just walk in and casually peruse the shelves... very hard indeed. One of the sweet little features of Reckless, and one that is consistently praised by all who visit the shop, is the fact that the staff take time to scribe a mini review of every release, which is attached to the sleeve on a sticker. Never overly enthusiastic, but just the right side of positive and informative, these stickers are an invaluable source of info for anyone shopping at Reckless, saving you having to ask staff a million and one questions and giving you more minutes (or hours) to continue your digging. Excellence on every level.

NORTH AMERICA

LEFT
Reckless has grown to be a successful mini chain, with three stores in Chicago. This is the Milwaukee Avenue branch.

A-1 Record Shop | New York City

What?	Hip hop, electronic, African, jazz, and more
Where?	439 East 6th Street, New York, NY 10009, USA
When?	1996
Why?	A digger's paradise with walls steeped in NYC history

A strong air of nostalgia flows through A-1 Records, one of New York's best-loved vinyl vendors. Once inside the door, you feel cocooned, comforted, and instantly at ease, thanks to a winning combination of a superlative music selection, a great atmosphere steeped in history, friendly staff, and a carefully curated and designed interior. So many of the shops in this book can lay claim to similar characteristics, yet they all have their own identity and A-1 is no different. Look up at the ceiling and you'll see a mass of color, a collage of lovingly arranged album covers, which means you're literally surrounded by music on all sides. The rows and rows of vinyl will have anyone who's even slightly interested in record collecting dribbling from the mouth. Within these horizontal stacks of black wax you will find a very broad collection of music, ranging from African sounds to jazz, spoken-word recordings to movie soundtracks.

It all started in 1996 when Isaac Kosman transferred his experience as a bookstore owner and flea-market regular into A-1 Records. The store was set up to offer an alternative to the more expensive vendors in the West Village and quickly became a go-to for a myriad of local and international artists, particularly some of NYC's most famous house music and hip-hop protagonists. Names such as Masters At Work, DJ Premier, The Alchemist, Tony Touch, and Pete Rock, plus many, many more, would spend hours trawling the shelves in search of records to sample and use in their productions. A-1 was intrinsic to both genres during that very fertile mid-1990s era, mostly thanks to its remarkable selection of rare groove, jazz, soul, and funk. Even today, many customers cite A-1 as being the best record store in the world, and there's no doubt that it is a total dream for those who bow down at the feet of the almighty acetate God.

A few insider tips: (1) try to avoid weekends as A-1 can get very packed; (2) if you're local, or in town for an extended period, try to go every few weeks when the stock will have had a full turnaround; and (3) it gets pretty hot in the summer, so be prepared. Other than that, for any other useful tidbits of information, you can always approach the A-1 team who are renowned for their eclectic knowledge and affable nature. Bossman Jay Delon, a long-term employee, works with his team (Seth, Jeremie, Mike, and Toshi) to ensure they're maintaining an inclusive policy with the music they sell. This is not a store that aims to cater to purists, and it benefits from this open-minded approach. A-1's legendary status has kept it afloat despite massive changes to the surrounding area in the last decade, and the hard work of the core team should help to secure its future for a long time to come.

BELOW
Records found in A-1 have supplied the breaks and samples for some of New York's most prestigious hip-hop producers.

The Thing | New York City

What?	**Lots of used vinyl in varying condition**
Where?	**1001 Manhattan Avenue, Brooklyn, New York 11222, USA**
When?	**1996**
Why?	**Dusty, squalid, and cluttered, but full of treasure for the ardent digger**

With its squalid basement setting, stacked with old records that have been ceremoniously dumped in this underground lair, The Thing's horror-flick-sounding name is actually quite fitting for some of its customers. Visitors who've never been there before take heed—it is a spot that takes a little bit of getting used to. It's quite dirty and unkempt, like a lot of the records it stocks, and probably a lot of the band members responsible for the recordings, too. But that is where this store's charm lies: it's so unpretentious. There's nothing about The Thing that is trendy or fashionable— it's a basement full of old records, pure and simple.

Set up in 1996 by Isaac Kosman, The Thing has become a firm favorite for diggers all over the Big Apple and way beyond the Hudson River, with fans from as far afield as Japan and Australia making the pilgrimage to Manhattan Avenue, in Brooklyn, to rummage through the extensive collection that lies beneath the bric-a-brac shop upstairs. South Americans make up a large percentage of the international customers, dropping in to grab old classics to sell in their own stores back home. Besides donations from people who want to give their collection a new lease of life, The Thing reaps the benefit of having New York sibling A-1 Records (see page 124) as its main supplier. Diggers delight in trawling through the offcuts they find in the dank basement, buoyed by the promise of finding gold in them thar hills. There are urban legends of customers finding ultra-rare pressings down there for less than a dollar, though how true these are remains to be confirmed. Whatever the truth, you'd better roll up your sleeves and prepare to get down and dirty. Indeed, to add to the "experience" of shopping at The Thing, none of the thousands of records is categorized—they are just lumped into crates, with a section for 12-inches, and that's it. This will be an ordeal for some and an exciting challenge for others, depending on your perspective. What makes it all a little easier to cope with is the fact that nothing costs more than $2, so you can easily leave with a big stack of wax without having to remortgage your house. The staff members enforce a sociable atmosphere, and the rules are that you must acknowledge other people working their way through the record boxes, even if it's just with a brief "Hello." You must also respect their personal space, and keep your piles of vinyl out of the narrow walkways, so that people can navigate their way around with ease. The Thing is a dream within a nightmare within a dream; just be patient and make sure you're prepared for its quirks.

Princeton Record Exchange | Princeton

What?	**Everything under the sun**
Where?	**20 South Tulane Street, Princeton, New Jersey 08542, USA**
When?	**1980**
Why?	**Big, friendly, and armed with a huge selection—it's a digger's dream**

One of the biggest record stores in America's Northeast, Princeton Record Exchange (or PREX to its friends) came into being in 1980, when Barry Weisfield founded the store as a base to sell his vinyl. Up until then, he'd spent five years trading at flea markets and selling LPs out of the back of his van (which he also slept in) at 27 campuses, from Dartmouth College, in New Hampshire, to American University in Washington. But Barry grew tired of being constantly on the move and so PREX was born on 20 Nassau Street.

After a few years, the business grew to the point where it needed new premises and the current location was secured in 1985. Measuring over 4,000 square feet (370 square meters) and home to more than 160,000 releases, it's one of those fabled record shops that seems to have everything you could ever want and music you didn't even know you wanted until you heard it or saw the album cover. The range is mouthwatering; you want several versions of the same classical composition with different conductors at the helm? You got it, and that's just the tip of the iceberg. The bargain bin is amazing; if you have a limited budget, it's just $1 per record and there are always (like, always) great releases to be had—it's just impossible to leave empty-handed.

Barry can usually be found hanging out at PREX ready to dole out advice, alongside the current owner and long-time manager, Jon Lambert. Barry sold the store to Jon in 2015, but retains a consultancy role, often helping out with purchasing collections. The massive venue isn't at all intimidating; on the contrary, the layout offers intimacy and comfort with a very astute attention to detail when it comes to the arrangement of the stock. You shouldn't have much trouble riffling through the boxes and shelves, but, if you do get a little confused, you can always holler for help. They have a great staff of 20, nine of whom have been working there for over 20 years. There are four assistant managers: Jeff J., the CD manager; Josh S., the DVD manager; Mark P., who handles much of the bookkeeping; and Amanda M., the counter manager. The main LP appraiser is Ben C., with Rob G. ably assisting. Fred S. oversees the "cheap" CDs; Mike W. handles the "cheap" DVDs; Laura S. is the assistant counter manager; Don R. is the main buyer of new merchandise; and Jim E. checks in all the new products and keeps the stacks organized. The store has achieved international recognition and it's easy to see why—there are very few of these treasure troves on our planet and even fewer that are as good at what they do.

BELOW
The turnover can be rapid at PREX, and customers often visit regularly knowing that they might find entirely new stock just a few days after their last visit.

Canada

Play De Record | Toronto

What?	**Dance 12-inches, reggae, and soca, plus DJ equipment and lessons**
Where?	**411 Spadina Avenue, Toronto, ON M5T 2G6, Canada**
When?	**1990**
Why?	**For the massive impact it's had on Toronto's electronic music scene**

Play De Record was opened by Eugene Tan and Jason Palma in 1990 in the traditional "Mom & Pop" mold—that is, independent, "family"-run, and committed to investing in the local community. The store's influence on Toronto's club scene has been profound, and it has become an essential mainstay for countless DJs and producers across the city and beyond for well over 20 years. Eugene and Jason's shop can be found in Spadina Avenue, one of the most prominent streets in this Canadian city, a spot they moved to in 2016 after spending over a quarter of a century on Yonge and Dundas.

PDR's strength lies in its superlative hip-hop stock, together with an exemplary selection of electronic music (house, techno, and a strong collection of deep dubstep and more UK-orientated sounds)—this puts it streets ahead of most of its competitors. Eugene's Trinidadian roots have led to a sizeable stock of soca, reggae, and other such Caribbean treasures, too. The shop's reputation has been built on its ability to deliver many rare and difficult-to-get-hold-of treats to several generations of record collectors, acting as a base for the city's DJ community, and helping to nurture its club culture. In the 1990s and early 2000s, you could pop in and find an assortment of flyers for events across the city, and new mixtapes from DJs and rappers based all over Canada and the US. As well as records, the store stocks DJ equipment such as turntables, synths, mixers, monitors, microphones, and so on.

Diversifying has kept PDR on an even keel, countering the effect of Napster and other such MP3 download sites, which saw a lot of record stores fall by the wayside. On top of that, budding DJs can sign up for lessons at Play De Academy, a DJ school set up in the shop's basement. Again, this endeavor has fed into Toronto's musical community, bolstering the scene and no doubt giving birth to a plethora of new talent. The decor is unfussy, with the music, DJ equipment, and merchandise doing the talking, rather than an overly fancy design. It's functional and makes shopping there a breeze. Being around for such a long time has cemented PDR's position as one of the city's most important cultural hubs. Eugene and his team are constantly analyzing the industry and customers' activity to make sure they're on trend, while also supporting new music and local artists. It's no mean feat, but they do it with passion, panache, and professionalism.

Atom Heart | Montreal

What?	Electronic 12-inches, left-field rock and indie, alternative, and much more
Where?	364 Sherbrooke Street East, Montreal, Quebec H2X 1E6, Canada
When?	1999
Why?	A contemporary institution in one of Canada's more culturally fertile cities

Atom Heart started selling records at the tail end of 1999 and quickly made its mark in Montreal, one of North America's most cosmopolitan cities. When you look at the volume of bands and musicians that have come out of Montreal, it's easy to see why this record shop has done so well and stayed in business since the dawn of the millennium. Arcade Fire, Grimes, Rufus Wainwright, Leonard Cohen, and a long list of other such world-renowned performers and recording artists all started out in this vibrant city.

Owners Raymond Trudel and Francis Gosselin met in the 1990s while working in a bookstore, spending most of their free time talking about music, movies, books, and other art forms. They were both buying huge amounts of special orders from local record shops and came to the conclusion that what they were listening to deserved a larger audience—and so, Atom Heart was born. The store allowed both men to deepen their love for music, share it with a wide audience, and dig even deeper into their respective genres; Raymond's tastes range from psych rock to shoegaze, post-punk, and experimental rock and electronics, whereas Francis was the typical 1990s bedroom DJ with a penchant for house, techno, RnB, funk of all kinds, the danceable side of post-punk, and experimental electronics. Nowadays, they employ two other staff members, Clevelan Cummings and Nico Serrus. Nico also DJs and produces, while Clevelan is a straight-up music enthusiast with diverse tastes—both men have a wide knowledge and are more than happy to share it with customers at Atom Heart.

ABOVE
Atom Heart offers a cozy sanctuary to cocoon local music lovers against those long Quebec winters.

The shop ended up at the center of several burgeoning scenes, as the open-door policy meant that local artists could sell their latest releases without any hint of a barrier to reaching their prospective audiences. Parallel to this, Montreal's premier electronic music festival MUTEK launched in the same year as Atom Heart. This led to an explosion of new electronic acts and labels across Canada, many of whom sold their music at the store. The shop itself is cozy and spacious, a home from home, where you feel free to hang out and chew the fat over the ins and outs of any music scene you care to mention, or anything else you may want to discuss with whoever is working there. Atom Heart remains at the epicenter of many of Montreal's concentric musical movements, and it's not uncommon for artists to meet for the first time there and go on to collaborate with one another. A crucial space in Montreal and one of the best vinyl stores in Canada.

RIGHT Tracks, Rio de Janeiro

Chapter Six

Caribbean, Central, and South America

6

Rockers International | Kingston

What?	**Reggae, dancehall, and a plethora of local and international releases**
Where?	**135 Orange Street, Kingston, Jamaica**
When?	**1976**
Why?	**The last remaining record store on Jamaica's infamous "Beat Street"**

In Jamaica, the birthplace of reggae, you'd think there would be plenty of record stores serving up the best in local music but, sadly, this is not the case. Back in the mid-1970s, when Rockers International was conceived, there were several other record shops on Orange Street. Located in downtown Kingston, the street was renamed "Beat Street" because of the dominance of vinyl outlets and the number of producers and performers who spent time there. It was at the heart of Kingston's music scene: legends Prince Buster and Dennis Brown were born on the street; Bob Marley's Tuff Gong International empire was founded there before it moved to Hope Road; Lee "Scratch" Perry's Upsetter Store was at the corner of Orange and Charles Street; and Coxsone Dodd had Muzik City there at 136d. Prince Buster's One Stop Record Shack, House of Music, and Unity Records were just a few of the shops that used to be located on the very same strip, while the mighty Augustus Pablo founded Rockers International there at 135 (where it still resides). In case you don't know, Augustus Pablo, or Horace Swaby as he was originally known, was a highly respected reggae producer and performer who passed away back in 1999. He was there at the birth of dub, bringing his own style to the groundbreaking reggae offshoot using the unmistakable sound of the melodica to assert his musical identity. The album *King Tubbys Meets Rockers Uptown*, which he produced and recorded in 1976, is widely acknowledged as one of the most important examples of dub music ever recorded.

Originally called Pablo Records Ltd., the shop took over the premises of Beverley's Ice Cream parlor, apparently the very same address where Dennis Emmanuel Brown was born in 1957. Back then, it specialized in dub and roots reggae, which set it apart from the other stores that once occupied premises on Orange Street—lots of the records sold there were Pablo's own or from his Rockers International label. The shop was taken over by Pablo's brother, Garth, in the 1980s, when the name was changed to Rockers International. Fast forward to the present day and it is the last remaining record store on the street, now recognized as a heritage site that maintains the legacy laid down by reggae's forefathers. The only other place in Jamaica that still sells vinyl is the legendary Randy's.

ABOVE
Rockers International logo appears on countless classic reggae and dub vinyls.

RIGHT
Legends of reggae look down at customers from the vintage posters that decorate the walls at Rockers International.

Ownership of the store remains within the Pablo family (his daughter, Isis Swaby; his son, Addis Pablo; and Karen Scott, Addis' mother), while day-to-day management and curation is handled by Ainsworth "Mitchie" Williams. In his youth Mitchie worked at Techniques Records on Chancery Lane with the late Winston Riley. After learning the trade there, he went on to do a couple of years at the infamous Randy's before moving to his current position at Rockers. As well as its superlative selection of reggae, dub, dancehall, and roots, from the 1960s up to the present day, Rockers also offers customers a chance to delve into Jamaica's rich musical history and now functions as a kind of museum, paying tribute to the ghosts of reggae's past. Visitors come from all over the world to downtown Kingston just to check it out. Mitchie is always at hand to offer knowledge and wisdom, whether it be recommending artists or trying to track down requests from eager diggers. A personal service is always available, to the point where Mitchie will do his utmost to procure signed copies of records if he's asked to, plus there's also a worldwide mail-order service on offer.

Inside the shop is a door featuring signatures from some of Jamaica's greats, plus a selection of records lined up on shelves and some stored away in black crates. Old posters adorn a couple of the walls, while there are CDs on display behind the glass front of the counter. On the counter, there's also an all-important fan blowing a cool breeze—essential for Jamaica's consistently hot weather. Across the road is a series of paintings, portraits of Augustus himself, Dennis Brown, and Gregory Isaacs (who had a cash and carry record store at 125 Orange Street, right next to Prince Buster's). Though the rest of the street is mostly occupied by furniture-makers, Rockers International keeps the reggae vibe alive. As an historical site it is hugely important, and one that represents a form of music that has had a massive global impact. Make sure you pay this one-of-a-kind location a visit.

Retroactivo Records | Mexico City

What?	**Rock, rock, rock, and lots more besides**
Where?	**Jalapa 125, Roma Nte., 06700 Mexico City, Mexico**
When?	**2004**
Why?	**To experience Mexican music at its best**

Opened on Christmas Eve, 2004, Retroactivo Records was one of the first stores of its kind in Mexico City. Sure, there had been plenty of record vendors in the city before, but Retroactivo took things to a whole other level. Launched by Alejandro Baeza and Claudio Pérez, the shop stocks over 50,000 records in the garage of an old house in one of the oldest neighborhoods in Mexico City. Due to its vintage look and appeal, you immediately feel as if you're in a time warp when you step through the front door. It's this kind of familiar atmosphere that aids the digging process no end. On top of this, everyone who works there (10 or so regular employees) has a friendly attitude, so you won't feel silly for asking questions. You'll be given invaluable advice, should you need it.

ABOVE
Retroactivo is also the home to its own vinyl pressing plant—how's that for commitment to wax?

Retroactivo specializes in rock, with a huge selection across the board, from soft rock and the more commercial stuff to older releases from some of the genre's legends. Besides that, you'll also find club music, hip hop, new beat, electronica, techno, high energy, jazz, avant-garde, Latin cuts, Dixieland, big band productions, and lots more, plus there's a big range of Mexican music: pop, rock, tropical, and contemporary. As one of the only places in the country with such a wide variety, Retroactivo attracts a diverse range of customers, with ages ranging from 12 to 70 and international diggers often popping in to trawl through the immense collection. Inside the store, all the records are protected in plastic sleeves and neatly arranged in their signature green crates. Fortunately, there is a distinction between English and Spanish recordings, so you won't end up searching for hours between various languages to find what you want. If you're on the street searching for the shop, look out for the tree outside with colored vinyl hanging from it. The front doors of the former garage space are adorned with paintings on the lower panels.

Retroactivo has diversified a tad and also sells turntables, audio equipment, plastic sleeves, and various other music-related paraphernalia. There may now be several other record stores in Mexico City vying for custom, but Retroactivo remains one of the city's true gems. It's a must for anyone who wants to spend quality time away from the hubbub to have a good dig around for precious acetate. Make sure you have some post-digging fish tacos at Chicojulio Fish Tacos & Chips just across the street—you won't regret it!

Discolombia | Barranquilla

What?	**African music, salsa, Palenque, champeta, and more**
Where?	**Cl. 36 #40–17, Barranquilla, Atlántico, Colombia**
When?	**1965**
Why?	**A grimy treasure chest that's full of Colombian gold**

Discolombia is a relic of days gone by in Barranquilla—a record shop standing alone as the sole remaining vinyl trader in a city that once had a plethora of record stores, many keen collectors, and a music scene that was teeming with activity. It is an important port, sitting where the Magdalena River meets the Caribbean Sea. This means the community there has a transient nature, and influences from the Caribbean and beyond have poured into the local culture. Barranquilla is lovingly referred to as the "Golden Gate of Colombia" because of its use as an entry point into Colombia. Ernesto Cortissoz International Airport, built in the city in 1919, was the first airport in South America and led to a further boost in international trade and tourism. This contributed to the local industry, with international DJs buying and trading records, playing music in clubs, and creating a melting pot of influences to inspire local artists, and Colombia as a whole.

Street parties are popular in Barranquilla, with sound systems set up, people drinking, dancing, singing, and socializing. The Carnival of Barranquilla is the most important folk and cultural festival in a country in which such celebrations are commonplace—it has been honored by UNESCO as a "Masterpiece of the Oral and Intangible Heritage of Humanity." With this vibrancy as a backdrop, in stepped Felix Butrón Senior, a music aficionado and canny businessman. He'd been successfully organizing concerts in his hometown, Magangué, and, off the back of that success, channeled his passion for music into buying a record store in the town back in 1962. Discolombia quickly grew and other branches were opened across the country—the Barranquilla store was inaugurated in 1965 and there were 17 outlets all over Colombia within a few of years. As times changed and music sales dwindled, Discolombia's team (which is now made up of the founder's son, Felix Butrón Junior, and his own son, Shane Butrón) had to close all their shops nationwide, only keeping the Barranquilla location open. Discolombia achieved great success through its stores and the highly influential label Felito Records, which was responsible for a series of hits in the 1970s. Butrón Senior's label supported the careers of acts such as Los Hermanos Sarmiento, Emilia Herrera, Esthercita Forero, La Niña Emilia, Petrona Martínez, Abelardo Carbonó, Adolfo Echeverría, Dolcey Gutiérrez, and others.

The shop itself is phenomenal, with shelves stacked high with records. It's pretty grimy, but therein lies its charm. Dog-eared sleeves belie the quality of the music sol, so look past their disheveled state and instead grab as much as you can. There is gold everywhere you turn: African music, salsa, Palenque, and champeta, plus lots of that glorious, local Afro-Colombian sound that transcends generations to fill everyone's life with energy and joy. With over 50,000 records, Discolombia houses one of the largest collections in the country, and new stock arrives all the time because Shane works with international distributors and local collectors to bolster the store's offerings. In a nation where radio is the main influence on people's listening habits, Discolombia represents freedom and independence, keeping the traditional folkloric recordings of the Latin nation alive—it is the beating heart of Colombia and the country would be lost without it.

CARIBBEAN, CENTRAL, AND SOUTH AMERICA

Casarão do Vinil | São Paulo

What?	**An extensive, eclectic selection**
Where?	**Rua dos Trilhos, 1212 - Mooca, São Paulo - SP, 03168-009, Brazil**
When?	**2014**
Why?	**To experience the wonder of a mansion full of records**

You can almost guarantee that a country as exotic and vibrant as Brazil will have a vinyl vendor that's extraordinary. The Casarão do Vinil ("big house of vinyl") contains over 700,000 records, plus a lot of vintage furniture, trinkets, paintings, clothing, books, and magazines. The beautiful, aging original decor of the house, which dates back to the 1940s, gives this space a totally unique and awe-inspiring character. Antique chandeliers hang from the ceilings, old furniture can be found in every room, and the paintwork is peeling away from the walls in places. Five dogs, the store's mascots, walk freely throughout the house; it really is a record outlet like no other. The huge mansion, which has around 6,500 square feet (604 square meters) of space, is intended by owner Manoel Jorge Dias to be a cultural hub. A former engineer who specialized in the controlled demolition of buildings across Brazil, Manoel (or Manezinho da Implosão, as he is also known) wanted Mooca, the neighborhood that's home to his infamous vinyl hoard, to be viewed as a center for music. Without a doubt, his endeavors have achieved just that, as his beloved Casarão do Vinil attracts attention from the world over.

You can find everything under the sun at this marvelous emporium, and Manoel is now knee-deep in the record-digging game. A latecomer to vinyl retail, he happened upon the hobby, which is now a vocation, by accident. Originally, he'd acquired a huge haul of bedding (via an auction) for a hostel he wanted to set up. As well as the bedding, there was also lots of women's clothing, which Manoel tried to sell on. Sales were poor and so he decided to offer customers the chance to exchange items for the clothing instead. He quickly accumulated paintings, books, furniture, and, eventually, vinyl. Manoel used the prospective hostel building to store all the wares he'd acquired and then, after an encounter with an impassioned customer who got so irate about the price of some records that he called the police, Manoel realized that demand for vinyl was still alive and well.

Manoel took charge of the building that houses Casarão do Vinil and brought in a team of people to organize and clean all the records – he now owns over a million, stored across three buildings. Finally, in March 2014, he opened the doors to his fantastical emporium, with a special vinyl fair that lasted for a weekend. After organizing a further 23 of these weekend events, Casarão was established as a permanent feature and has become a hugely popular stop-off for local collectors and enthusiasts from every corner of the globe. Manoel says that they sometimes have up to 700 people trawling the boxes and shelves at weekends, and he once sold 18,000 records in a single weekend. One of the world's most fascinating record vendors, Casarão do Vinil is a beguiling, jaw-dropping, magical space that has established itself as a cultural center in a very short space of time. Incredible.

Tropicália Discos | Rio de Janeiro

What?	**MPB, baby!**
Where?	**Praça Olávo Bilac, 28 - Centro, Rio de Janeiro - RJ, 20041-010, Brazil**
When?	**2003**
Why?	**For an unparalleled insight into Brazilian music**

Unlike Japan, CDs didn't do as well in Brazil. This meant that Márcio Rocha, who owned a music shop selling CDs, needed to find a new avenue—and so, in 2003, Tropicália Discos was born. Set up with his business partner, Bruno Alonso, the outlet allowed Márcio to channel his passion for music and records into a space that would become one of Rio's best-loved musical hubs. It is the place to go for MPB (*Música Popular Brasileira* or "Brazilian Popular Music") in all its many incarnations. For the uninitiated, MPB is an amalgamation of many different styles of music, all united under the umbrella of Brazilian pop music—it comes in so many different varieties, from jazz and bossa nova to samba, soul, and disco. Tropicália Discos has adopted an unrelenting policy to support and showcase the music, resulting in an entire wall of the store dedicated to the multifaceted genre. If you don't know much about it, worry not; the section is very well organized and labeled in such a way so as not to be intimidating. If you're still stumped by a slew of names and labels you've never heard of, then turn to Márcio who will gladly guide you through the entire history of the music, should you so wish, or at least supply you with some priceless nuggets of information to help you make an informed choice. Plus, he'll pull out those hard-to-get-hold-of releases for the MPB diehards. The rest of the store contains jazz, soul, funk, and a ton of US imports, all at the kind of prices that will have you leaving with half the shop's stock.

ABOVE
With 30,000 records in stock, you can almost certainly spend a whole day here, so strap yourself in and prepare for a lengthy dig.

Tropicália Discos sits at the center of Brazil's hugely popular music scene, with the staff not only pushing modern MPB releases, but also doing a huge amount of digging themselves in order to uncover rare releases and give them a new lease of life via the shop's immense YouTube channel. So far, there are around 800 uploads and counting... a crucial source of Brazilian music for fans all over of the world. If you can't make it to Brazil, then you can always take advantage of their mail-order service and have fresh MPB delivered to your door. Tropicália Discos has become one of the world's most important curators of Brazilian music, accumulating a staggering number of records and introducing fans all over the globe to the vibrant sounds of this South American nation. An amazing place, with priceless historical and cultural value.

Tracks | Rio de Janeiro

What?	**Music, art, cinema, and books**
Where?	**Praça Santos Dumont, 140-Gávea, Rio de Janeiro - RJ, 22470-060, Brazil**
When?	**1997**
Why?	**Impeccable selection and a cozy atmosphere**

Tracks was founded in 1997 by three friends—the trio were music-lovers and serious record collectors. At the time, they regarded the music scene in Rio as very poor; the media was dominated by low-quality music, appealing to the lowest common denominator and pushed by major labels to make a quick buck. The trio's idea was to create a space that was totally different to anything else going on in the city, to counteract this proliferation of trashy music. The first step was the installation of their store in Gávea, which is one of the most interesting neighborhoods in Rio and located between Jardim Botanico and Leblon Beach. Tracks was set up in the heart of the so-called "Baixo Gávea," a square full of bars and restaurants, plus an art gallery, a small experimental theater, and a nightclub. It's a bohemian district where intellectuals used to gather to muse on art, life, and philosophy, and is well worth exploring while you're in the area.

Initially, the musical focus was a fusion of the tastes and knowledge of the three partners: classic rock, jazz, alternative Brazilian music, and the best collection of world music in the city. Since opening, Tracks has only had nine employees, which means the team knows the shop inside out—in fact, the manager has been there since the very beginning. The level of expertise is unsurpassed, and you can expect a thoroughly personal and consistently courteous service when you walk through the doors. This is one of those record vendors that oozes professionalism and does it with style; the interior is slick and polished, though also cozy and homely—you can grab a book and kick back for a bit, chatting with the staff and befriending other customers. Tracks has an effortless feel; it's classy and switched on to modern culture in an unpretentious way. Doubling up as a bookstore, you'll find the vinyl section upstairs. The selection has now been bolstered by a wide range of genres, on top of the music adored by the founding partners. Not long after they launched, the Tracks team linked up with a supplier of imported records offering a good amount of electronic music on consignment for testing. Their electronic section caught the attention of journalists and DJs, and a whole new bunch of record collectors was soon flocking around the store.

Through the ups and downs of the Brazilian economy and the transformation of the phonographic market, the original trio broke up, leaving only one of the founders, Heitor Trengrouse. Over time the shop solidified its position as a focal point for Rio's more alternative music scene and added new products such as exclusive T-shirts, objets d'art, handicrafts, and street art, mostly produced by people who frequent the store. Since the beginning, everyone involved in Tracks has worked tirelessly to maintain the initial philosophy, which is to provide the very best music in a welcoming and chilled environment.

ABOVE
With shelf space dedicated to the best in music, art, film, and literature, Tracks is a cultural cornerstone in the Brazilian capital.

CARIBBEAN, CENTRAL, AND SOUTH AMERICA

Eureka Records | Buenos Aires

What?	**Argentinian rock, indie, and dance, plus a huge selection of international releases**
Where?	**Defensa 1281, C1143AAA San Telmo, Buenos Aires, Argentina**
When?	**1999**
Why?	**Argentina's very best record outlet**

Argentina is the home of tango, the sultry dance that electrifies and dazzles in equal measure. The accompanying music has become one of the country's greatest exports, inspiring dancers all over the world and producing artists such as Carlos Gardel, Ástor Piazzolla, Juan d'Arienzo, Arminda Canteros, and Rodolfo Biagi. The nation's folk music and its own rock, indie, and pop acts all take great pride in the music they produce and carry a rich history in everything they do. Argentina's heady mix of European and South American cultures results in a dynamic and prolific music industry.

Eureka Records is the biggest record store in Buenos Aires, the capital of Argentina, and perhaps in the whole country. It is nestled among the cafés, galleries, and tango parlors of San Telmo, a bustling barrio (the oldest in Argentina) where you'll see artists and dancers plying their trade and performing in the streets. Eureka's story begins in 1999 with a music-lover called Alberto Malosetti. Down on his luck and broke, Alberto made the difficult decision to start selling his personal record collection in order to keep his head above water. Working out of an antique shop owned by a friend, he did his best to keep himself afloat, though it didn't quite work out because vinyl was not as popular then as it is now. Instead, Alberto found that having a "store" meant he could pick up records for ridiculously low prices (and often for nothing), as many Argentinians were abandoning vinyl for digital formats. As he acquired more and more records, word began to spread about his darkened corner in San Telmo that sells great albums. The vinyl fanatics of the city started to frequent the shop and became Alberto's friends. Eureka was alive, and it remains a testament to the hard work and belief of Señor Malosetti.

A lot of the music sold at Eureka is local, which is great for those who want to discover new homegrown talent or really delve into Argentina's history. Alongside all that good stuff, you'll also find global sounds, ranging from disco to funk, over to rock and new wave. The spot is now co-run by Alberto's son, Ignacio, who invests the same level of devotion in every facet of Eureka as his father, having spent much of his youth there soaking up the atmosphere and learning about music firsthand. (Note: Ignacio's best friend, Leo, also mans the counter.) Ignacio carries on his father's legacy with a staunch belief in the value of physical products, while cultivating a space in which people want to spend quality time with the records and get acquainted with fellow devotees of the vinyl Goddess. Besides the shop being handed down from father to son, the only other major change has been its location—a short jaunt down the street, which happened eight years ago. Everything else remains true to the store's core ethos—why change anything when it works so stupendously well?

LEFT
Elvis lives in Argentina! Well, a cardboard version does, at least.

BELOW
Wall-to-wall records—just the way vinyl junkies like it.

CARIBBEAN, CENTRAL, AND SOUTH AMERICA

Index

Acknowledgments

Thanks to everybody who has contributed to the making of this book. To my partner in crime for her unwavering support and positivity, and all my friends and family, especially my nan who's always been there for me and my mum for planting the musical seed in the first place.

Marcus Barnes is a music journalist, copywriter, and editor who grew up in a house full of vinyl, thanks to his mum's love of reggae. He is currently Techno Editor at *Mixmag* and Creative Director of Don't Lose The Magic, with numerous other freelance projects on the go. Marcus has contributed to an exhaustive list of renowned publications—including *The Observer*, *The Independent*, *Time Out London*, *i-D*, *Clash*, and many more—regularly traveling the world to investigate music scenes from Beirut to Montreal, attending festivals, and interviewing musicians. He is the author of global festival guide *Around The World In 80 Raves* and transformative festival journal *TRANSFORM*. Marcus is based in south-east London, UK.